Tabasco the Saucy Raccoon

Lyn Hancock

Illustrations by Loraine Kemp

sononis
PRESS
WINLAW BRITISH COLUMBIA

Copyright © 2006 by Lyn Hancock
Interior illustrations © 2006 by Loraine Kemp

Library and Archives Canada Cataloguing in Publication
Hancock, Lyn, 1938-
    Tabasco the saucy raccoon / Lyn Hancock ; illustrated by Loraine
Kemp.
ISBN 1-55039-156-9
    1. Raccoons—Biography—Juvenile literature. 2. Raccoons as
pets—Juvenile literature. 3. Hancock, Lyn, 1938– —Juvenile literature.
I. Kemp, Loraine II. Title.
QL795.R15H35 2006   j636.976'32'0929   C2006-900693-8

Sono Nis Press most gratefully acknowledges the support for our
publishing program provided by the Government of Canada through the
Book Publishing Industry Development Program (BPIDP), the Canada
Council for the Arts, and the British Columbia Arts Council.

Edited by Laura Peetoom
Copy edited by Dawn Loewen
Interior illustrations by Loraine Kemp
Cover and interior design by Jim Brennan
Cover and interior photos courtesy of the author

Published by
Sono Nis Press
Box 160
Winlaw, BC V0G 2J0
1-800-370-5228

books@sononis.com
www.sononis.com

Distributed in the U.S. by
Orca Book Publishers
Box 468
Custer, WA 98240-0468
1-800-210-5277

Printed and bound in Canada by Friesens

The Canada Council | Le Conseil des Arts
for the Arts | du Canada

To my sister Jan, my parents Ted and Doris Taylor, and my animal loving nieces Julie and Sarah and cousin Melita

CHAPTER ONE

THERE'S A RACCOON IN MY PARKA

"Two tickets to Toronto, please, for me and my pet raccoon," I said to the lady at the Air Canada ticket counter in Vancouver. I tried to sound nonchalant, as if this were something I asked for every day. She looked up, startled, then drew back in alarm as I placed a wooden box in front of her.

"I know he has to go in the baggage compartment," I continued. "So I brought my own carrying case—unless, of course, you want me to use yours."

My parents had brought me to the airport early this Sunday morning, and, as expected, the terminal was almost deserted. Still, Dad couldn't help looking embarrassed. He and Mom were visiting me from Australia and, once again, they were being dragged into one of their daughter's "crazy" schemes. "When will you ever grow up?" my mother would often sigh. She looked at the agent apologetically.

The lady behind the ticket counter stared at the box as if any minute it might explode. I felt that if she'd been a bank teller she would have reached for an alarm. "Where is your...your raccoon?" she asked fearfully, not really believing that I had one.

"Here," I said, reaching into the pocket of my parka and pulling out a red woollen toque. "Meet Tabasco."

The lump of grizzled fur snuffling sleepily into the wool in the palm of my hand looked more like a pin cushion than a one-pound, week-old, orphaned raccoon.

The airline lady's manner changed. "Oh, it's just a baby," she crooned. "It's adorable." Then, remembering where she was, she looked horrified. "You can't put that little raccoon in the baggage compartment, it's too tiny. It might die!"

"Then what do you suggest?" I asked innocently.

The ticket agent's voice dropped suddenly. Looking quickly behind her to make sure nobody was listening, she whispered, "Wrap it up in a blanket and pretend it's your baby."

Now it was my turn to look horrified. I certainly had a baby and I was carrying a bag of baby supplies—bottle, formula, vitamins, towels and, yes, a blanket too—but somehow I couldn't bring myself to take Tabasco through security as a human baby.

I thanked the lady, bought a ticket to Toronto for one, stuffed the raccoon's travelling box into my suitcase, watched while it sailed away on the conveyor belt and shepherded my poor parents through the terminal.

"Tabasco's got to go to Toronto with me," I told them as we had coffee in the cafeteria. "So I'll just carry him in the pocket of my parka. He's small enough to fit into my hand. He'll be no trouble." My parents just scratched their heads.

My plan would not work nowadays when airport security measures are so strict. Now you have to take off your coat and sometimes even your shoes before you pass through the gate.

"This is the last call for Air Canada flight 960 to Toronto."

"Lynette!" My father's voice broke into the announcement with the tone I remembered as a child. "YOU'RE GOING TO MISS YOUR PLANE."

"Come and say goodbye to me at security."

We rushed to the gate. In one hand I carried a shopping bag of raccoon baby supplies and my purse overloaded with books, schedules, pens, pencils, a diary and a camera. In the other I cuddled the baby raccoon. In the big, droopy parka pocket he was just like a joey kangaroo in a pouch.

"People will be wondering why you are carrying both bags in one hand," Mom whispered worriedly as we ran.

"And why you are holding your coat out sideways," added Dad. "Talk about a one-armed bandit."

"I want to let the parka swing freely so Tabasco won't be bumped," I whispered back.

My heart was thumping. Ahead lay the X-ray machines and if I continued on course the girl standing beside them would be on my left side, Tabasco's side. In case she wondered why I suddenly veered to the right, I swung around on the spot, waved to my parents with my left hand and changed direction. Smiling sweetly at the attendants, I hefted my two bags onto the conveyor belt with my right hand. "See you in a couple of weeks," I called to Mom and Dad. "Enjoy Vancouver and the apartment, okay?"

They would probably spend the whole time worrying. But they'd be worrying more if they had to babysit Tabasco, I thought, as I dashed through the doors of the plane as they were closing.

"May I take your coat?" asked the flight attendant, leading me quickly towards my seat.

It was almost the middle of May, with warm spring weather. I knew I looked silly wearing my arctic parka, even if it was only the outer shell.

"Are you all right?" she asked. "You look as if you have a cold coming on. Do you need Gravol or an Aspirin?"

"No, I think I'll be okay. They gave me a seat by the washroom. I may have to use it a lot."

My two companions in the middle and window seats looked sympathetic. From the way I perched on the right-hand side of my aisle seat, leaving the left for the raccoon, I must have looked as if there were something wrong with my hip or buttocks.

"I'm Pam, I'm going to Detroit," chirped the buxom, grey-haired lady beside me. "Here, put one of your bags under my seat. You seem to be carrying a lot."

She didn't know the half of it. It was time for Tabasco's two-hourly feed but he still seemed to be sleeping, so I chattered back to the lady. Perhaps I would need her to stay friendly.

"I'm Lyn Hancock and I'm going to Toronto to begin

a promotion tour for my latest book," I explained as I pulled down the table in front of me. "It sounds silly but I haven't had time to read it myself."

"*There's a Raccoon in My Parka,* hmmm!" she said, reading the title. "And that's you and the raccoon right there—on the front cover. I like animals." She sighed. "But I had to leave my cat with the babysitter. They don't allow animals on planes, you know, at least not in economy class."

I was still perched on the edge of the seat and I stiffened even more. This was not the kind of talk I wanted.

Pam chatted on. "But weren't you afraid of the raccoon at first?"

"No..." I wanted to change the subject.

"I guess when they're babies, they're fine."

With that, Tabasco chittered a couple of times and started to move around in the toque. Quickly, I put my hand in my pocket, gave him a little squeeze and let him suck on my thumb. He would be fine stretching out the length of my hand but I was already starting to get cramped. "Excuse me," I said. "I've got to go to the washroom."

Fortunately, the flight attendants clattering dishes in the galley outside the toilet made more noise than Tabasco's wake-up calls. I rushed inside, hung Tabasco on the door in my parka and sat on the seat while I sorted through his supplies. His milk bottle was still warm from when I had prepared the formula back at the apartment but I boosted its temperature by running it under the hot water tap. Then I uncurled Tabasco from his red toque.

I shoved a nipple into the furry ball that looked more a rat than a raccoon. Not that Tabasco was much interested in drinking. To stimulate his appetite and keep him sleepy for the rest of the trip I sat him on the floor for some exercise.

Tabasco was still a blob—"a macaroon," my mother said, "not a raccoon." His eyes were still closed, his ears were still flattened and he had a round snout and chubby cheeks. But even at a week old, he was clearly a raccoon—black-ringed tail, the black crosspiece on his forehead that would one day be a mask, and those human-like hands.

"Yes, Tabasco, you're a cute baby."

He waddled towards my voice and, with his tail swishing from side to side, started to climb my leg. A quick cuddle, a slow intake of an ounce of milk, and I put him back on the floor, this time for a rear-end massage so that he could clear his bowels. I did not want any "accidents" in the cabin, especially at mealtime.

After letting him scuffle around on the floor for a few more minutes, I put him back in my parka pocket and dropped a tissue on his head.

Back in my seat, I ordered an orange juice, and the flight attendant glanced at my book. "A raccoon in your parka, eh? Very interesting!" Later, when he returned with another juice, he said, "And something for the raccoon?" Did he guess?

Tabasco was born in the attic of a house in the Kerrisdale section of Vancouver. His mother had moved in on Easter weekend, knocking out some boards in the backyard fence, climbing to the roof from a twenty-foot cedar tree and ripping out half a dozen cedar shakes. And, there in the cozy crawl space beside a warm chimney, she had given birth to Tabasco and his brothers and sisters.

Mr. and Mrs. Rowles were irate. This was the second time their house had been invaded by pesky raccoons. Unlike some of their neighbours, they always closed their compost bins, sealed their garbage cans and never left food around on their porch. Yet twice it had cost them over a thousand dollars to fix the damage from raccoons. They told the newspaper that they feared the invaders might bite their children.

Mr. Rowles had replaced the shakes, hung out socks stuffed with mothballs, cut branches from the cedar tree, but nothing deterred the raccoons. He had complained to the city pound, the Society for the Prevention of Cruelty to Animals, the Association for the Protection of Fur-Bearing Animals, the Fish and Wildlife Branch. He'd asked advice from a pest control company.

"Most of them were sympathetic but nobody helped," said Mrs. Rowles with a sigh. "Trouble is, baby raccoons are such dear little things that nobody, including us, wants to hurt them."

There were two sides to the story. Some people loved raccoons and other people hated raccoons. One person asked the Fish and Wildlife people to go around and give eye drops to all the wild raccoons in her area. Another person vowed he'd shoot the next coon to swing in his corn patch. A local radio station got in the middle and ran a contest asking listeners for ways to rid themselves of unwanted raccoons.

"Paint your roof with Tabasco sauce," said the person who won. "It's such hot stuff no raccoon will ever put his paws past it."

A little Tabasco sauce goes a long way, but Mr. and Mrs. Rowles didn't try this suggestion. Instead, they asked the Children's Zoo to come and remove the litter of raccoons from their attic. Now the zoo had the problem. It had too many raccoons. It tried to release unwanted raccoons into the wild, but as more and more people moved into wilderness areas, there was less room for raccoons—or bears or cougars or all the other animals that the officials called "problem wildlife." The zoo could display baby animals for a while and use them to teach people to appreciate and conserve their natural habitat, but they had a problem when the babies grew up.

I closed my eyes and thought back to all the orphaned animals that had been brought to my doorstep in Vancouver and Victoria when I had been married to a wildlife biologist. Sam, the sick fur seal pup who had not been able to survive the fur seals' annual migration down to California from Alaska but had washed ashore near my home. Tom, Oola, Lara and Tammy, the four cougar kittens whose mother had been shot by a hunter and who had been sold to an old lady unable to keep them. Gypsy, the gibbon ape whose own mother in the Tacoma Zoo had thrown her away at birth and broken her arm. Bubu and Edward, the black bears whose den had been crushed by loggers and whose mother had run away. Rocky, the raccoon whose mother was shot for killing ducks and goldfish near people who preferred ducks and goldfish. And Scarlett the macaw, Pierretta the Canada goose, Pixie and Pete the coatimundis. Porky the porcupine, Baldy the bald eagle. And still more orphans who had lived with me at the Wildlife Conservation Centre near Victoria, British Columbia.

And now there was Tabasco. I had decided, after my husband gave up both his career as a biologist and our marriage and I found myself suddenly alone, that I would go into the wilds myself and study cougars. So there I was at Simon Fraser University in Burnaby, enrolled in a graduate program and living in a no-pet apartment on the third floor. Well, it wasn't quite a no-pet apartment. The lease read "No cats or dogs."

As soon as I moved in, certain animals moved in too—by themselves. Honest! First, there were the starlings who made a nest on the balcony. Then there was a one-legged gull who came each day to sit on the railing. Then there were the pigeons who came right inside and laid eggs in the back of the defunct TV set. They were all good company as I sat night and day with my books. But I missed having a close companion of my own.

So when the Children's Zoo phoned to ask if I would like to look after one of the raccoons who had raided the Kerrisdale attic, I accepted. "Just don't put it out in the wild or we'll have another problem," they warned.

It was the right time. I was studying not only cougars and other predators but people's attitudes towards them. Why did people like some animals and not others?

One of the problems in taking on a wild animal pet, especially one as rambunctious as a raccoon, is where to keep it and what to do with it when it grows up. Often people invite animals into their homes as pets and then can't stand the pressure when they demand round-the-clock attention, not only when they're young but also when they're grown up. Raccoons are very adaptable but they hate being caged. Fortunately, my other raccoon, Rocky, had never been caged. He'd been free to travel with me all around Alaska, Yukon and British Columbia in a truck and a boat and then he'd gone to live on one of the privately owned Gulf Islands near Victoria.

I promised the zoo I wouldn't release Tabasco, at least not in an urban area where he could become a nuisance like his mother. I intended to keep Tabasco forever. When my school days were over I planned to live with him on an island of my own.

Mom and Dad arrived in Vancouver just about the time I picked up Tabasco from the zoo. I slept in my office on a camp cot and gave my parents the big bedroom in my apartment. They were Aussies and adventurous types who had camped with me all over Europe and North America. I felt sure they would be able to handle a raccoon. But I came home from late-night lectures a couple of times to find notes like this on the table:

> Lynette,
> Raccoon had half his bottle about 8 p.m. then wet in the corner on paper and bit my toes through the socks until I had to cuff him on the ear.
> Your obedient servant,
> Dad

P.S. from your other obedient servant: 12:40 a.m. Can't manage your baby any longer. Milk all over me. I think baby just wants to play and I have to keep the bathroom lights on.
All yours,
Mom

There was obviously no way I could leave Tabasco with my parents for the time I would be in Toronto.

So there we were on the plane going east with permission to travel across every province on my tour except Alberta. "People in Alberta are not allowed to have wild animals in their possession unless they belong to a recognized zoo or a licensed game farm," warned my friend at British Columbia's Fish and Wildlife Branch. "Alberta is very, very sticky about that."

But my other friend Jack, who worked for the same branch, said, "I know bureaucrats. I am one myself. No one in his right mind would object to a raccoon visiting a province for two days. Just write to the director in Alberta and tell him what you are going to do and where you are going to be."

"But perhaps I should let him know that Tabasco is a B.C. raccoon not an Albertan raccoon, that it wasn't born in the wild but in a house, that it really belongs to the Children's Zoo and I'm just borrowing him for a while to teach people about wildlife, that I'm experienced in wild animal care..."

"Lyn, stop it. Write just as I tell you. In fact, I'll write the letter for you. I'll ask the director to mail your permit to your last hotel before Alberta."

And so Jack wrote the letter and made a carrying case for Tabasco the night before we caught the plane.

"We are now on our descent to Toronto. Would you fasten your seat belts and make sure your tables and seats are in the upright position."

The voice of the flight attendant cut into my reverie. Amazingly, Tabasco had slept right through the four-hour flight.

When we reached the baggage terminal, Carolynn from the publishing house was waiting at the gate. "I didn't know if I'd be taking you to the hotel or to prison," she laughed nervously. "Where's the raccoon?"

"In my pocket. But it's time for his bottle. Let's get to the hotel. I'll introduce you in the taxi."

CHAPTER TWO

THERE'S A RACCOON ON MY PROMOTION TOUR

A promotion tour for a new book is always hectic, as publicists with authors in tow or authors alone clutching maps and schedules race madly around to radio and television stations, newspaper and magazine offices, restaurants and bookstores. There can be breakfast interviews, lunch interviews and dinner interviews where you are so busy answering questions you have no chance to eat your meal; there can be days when you are so busy tearing around trying to be on time you have no meals at all. And then at the end of the day you have to pack your suitcase, gather up your books, take a taxi to the airport and fly off to another city where it all happens again. As the days and the cities go by, the studios, the offices, the corridors and the reporters all begin to look the same. Whatever you say on the first day sets the pattern for whatever you will say on the rest of the days.

In my case, I compound the problem by adding visits to schools and libraries, lectures to groups such as natural history societies, and research sessions at universities.

Knowing that people of all ages remember a message better if the messenger is interesting, I like to take along an animal or two. Sam the seal, Rocky the raccoon, Tom and his sister cougars, Bubu the bear, Bun Bun the varying hare, Ludwig, Gomer and Ponderosa the tortoises and the rest of the crew at our Wildlife Conservation Centre have inspired both kids and adults to become naturalists, zoologists, biologists, veterinarians, writers, broadcasters or aware conservationists.

At this stage in his life, Tabasco appealed to everybody. Desks were emptied and microphones abandoned whenever I took him out of his toque and totebag. "May I touch him?" was always the first question. Even busy businessmen in pinstripe suits loved Tabasco. One CBC producer hurriedly ordered a taxi to bring her children to the studio before we left.

"You know," said Carolynn in surprise one day, "that TV interviewer today didn't even mind when Tabasco started to squawk on the show and threatened to drown him out on the air. And I nearly died when the raccoon defecated among the lipsticks on Irma's makeup table, but she didn't seem to mind a bit."

A famous writer once said that if a domestic animal loves you, it becomes your slave, but if a wild animal loves you, you become its slave. And so it was with Tabasco. He didn't open his eyes till we were two days into the tour and even then he had a pretty blurred view of the world. It was two weeks or more before he did much else than sleep between two-hour and then four-hour feeds. He was just a tiny fluffball snuffling into my toque or wobbling around on his delicate hands and feet, but he was surrounded daily by a retinue of adoring slaves.

Secretaries strained his formula. Makeup girls minded him while I discussed the program. Salesmen weighed him on post office scales. Receptionists bathed him in bathroom sinks. Technicians encouraged him to exercise on the office floor and stood guard in case anybody stepped on him. Messenger boys scurried around looking for cups, warm water and paper towels. Other guests ran out of the studio to fetch supplies like baby oil for his dry skin. And busy hosts and hostesses cuddled him to sleep.

Despite the extra work and the many times interviews scheduled for fifteen minutes stretched into thirty minutes or even an hour, causing frantic phone calls and taxi rides, Carolynn was enchanted. I heard her describing some of the highlights to her cohorts at Doubleday.

"Do you know that I have to bring a fresh egg to work every morning for Tabasco's bottle—and hope that it doesn't break all over my new purse? And yesterday I had to rush out to the Bay and buy a pair of nylons to strain the formula because the egg was too thick to go through the nipple! You should have seen the look on the faces of the clerk and the other customers when I ripped open the package at the counter, stretched the stocking over a cup and poured in the mixture."

Tabasco had Carolynn and plenty of other caretakers during the day. At night back at the hotel, I left him in the bathroom while I flew down to the floor that had ice cubes, shovelled a bucketful out of the box and ran back to the room to keep his milk bottle cold between feeds. It was unseasonably hot that week in Toronto, so I usually stored his formula (Enfalac or evaporated milk laced with egg yolk and multivitamins) on the open window ledge of my room, buried in ice.

After a day of rushing around in my parka and sitting under hot studio lights in stage makeup, I threw off my shoes and stockings as soon as I hit the hotel room, and changed into something loose and comfortable before I buzzed the elevator. There were often double takes from the better dressed business types as I whizzed in and out of elevators in bare feet carrying my ice cubes and milk bottles. "How's your baby?" some of them would say to start a conversation. "Fine, thank you, but it happens to be a raccoon," I'd reply, but not stay long enough to see their reaction.

By the time we hit Winnipeg, Tabasco was nearly three weeks old and had gained a couple of pounds. His eyes were open, he could dig his claws into things and climb up furniture and stockinged legs, and he wobbled around now after eating rather than going to sleep. He was developing quite a voice. To his "wuff, wuff, wuff" that said, "I like this nice warm stuff going down my throat" or "Now, how can I make myself comfortable?" he had added a strident, piercing trill that said, "I'm hungry" or "I'm lost" and a startled, rasping growl that said, "What's wrong? What's happening? Who are you?" Most of the time, though, he kept in contact with me by various kinds of chittering and I learned to communicate with him by chittering back.

With a couple of hours to spare before we caught our plane out of Winnipeg, I took a taxi to visit Con and Dime Reilly in their beautiful riverside mansion. "You'd better mind your manners, Tabasco," I admonished the raccoon.

Like most people, Dime thought he was cute, and even Con, who confessed to liking ducks more than raccoons, was impressed. Nevertheless, I decided to play it safe and keep Tabasco outside on the Reillys' front lawn. He knew how to climb. He knew how to walk—backwards, that is. Now in his first long foray through grass he learned how to walk forwards. No longer did he just bumble around, he was beginning to have a mind—and a direction—of his own.

To this baby raccoon, the lawn must have looked like a forest. I thought that giving him plenty of exercise would tire him out and keep him quiet on the plane. But it had the opposite effect. He waddled around in the grass and climbed up Dime's stockings, Con's pant legs and my pantsuit. His long claws didn't do much damage to our skin but I couldn't say the same for nylon, polyester and silk. Then, because of the excitement perhaps, he developed diarrhea, which oozed down Con's arms when he picked him up for the ride to the airport.

Fortunately, we were still friends when I and my chittering raccoon said goodbye in the terminal. "Tabasco, shut up, tell me about it later. Right now I have to take you on another plane ride," I whispered into the totebag en route to the airport washroom.

But he kept on chittering. I sat on the toilet seat and

gave him his bottle. But he wasn't interested in drinking; he had found his legs, all four of them, and he wanted to explore the floor beyond the door. "Come back," I said, trying to keep my voice down and my raccoon hidden from curious people in the next cubicles. His inquisitive nose was just poking out into the main bathroom area when I managed to lean forward from my precarious position atop the toilet seat, scoop him up and pop him back in the bag.

Time was ticking away and passengers were already on board. We couldn't wait any longer. Despite Tabasco's protests, I transferred him to the pocket of my parka with my hand for company and let him expend his newfound energy by exercising his teeth instead of his legs. Fortunately, he stopped chittering as we swung through security.

But what would happen on the plane? He was still excited by his experience at the Reillys'. This time he wasn't satisfied to stay sleeping in the totebag. He climbed out of my pocket, crept behind my back and started to crawl to the seats next to ours. Thank goodness we had a whole row to ourselves. I feigned sleep every time the flight attendant came by. And to keep her away, I even went without dinner! How far does one go to protect a stowaway raccoon?

I was about to find out. The ominous-looking envelope awaiting us under the door of our last hotel room in Saskatchewan was not the permit that Jack had requested. It was a letter from Alberta's Fish and Wildlife forbidding me to bring Tabasco into the province at all.

"What shall I do with you, my pet?" I asked the raccoon as we went to bed. "Send you home alone in the baggage compartment to British Columbia on another plane? Let you loose in Saskatchewan?"

Tabasco chattered a reply and snuggled into my pillow. He preferred to take his chances with me.

I was very nervous the next morning as I stepped off the plane in Calgary. Tabasco was on his best behaviour, sleeping quietly in my pocket. No uniformed officer approached so I hailed a taxi and headed for our appointment at the radio station.

The taxi driver had the radio on, tuned to CBC. "Today we have a special visitor on the program: Tabasco, a saucy raccoon," I heard. "Join us in half an hour to welcome Tabasco and his companion."

When we arrived at the station I explained the situation. The host agreed not to say that Tabasco was in the studio. I told the audience stories about raccoons but I didn't confess that one of them was sleeping by the microphone in front of me.

Our next appointment was at the TV studio, where twenty-five children were sitting in a circle eagerly awaiting Tabasco. They stared in awe as they carefully passed my little raccoon from hand to hand around the ring.

The interviewer didn't tell her viewers that Tabasco was in an Alberta studio. When they saw Tabasco he was lying on a red rug and when they saw me I was wearing my blue skirt. What they didn't know was that whenever the cameraman wanted a shot of me, the interviewer would whisk Tabasco and his red rug away from my knees. To the viewers at home, it looked as if I had brought Tabasco on film but not in person. They never saw us together.

The reporter at the newspaper was so impressed with Tabasco that she put his photo on the front page. But she didn't say where the photograph was taken. Nobody knew that it was taken just outside her office. To get to know Tabasco better she took us to lunch. I stashed the raccoon under the table, but she couldn't resist taking him out of the totebag and holding him when I left to make a phone call. "He snuffles and squeaks till he goes to sleep, just like a fussy baby," she said in surprise when I returned to the table.

By this time Tabasco was drinking three or four ounces of milk four times a day, he weighed four pounds and he was too big even for the totebag. On the plane back to Vancouver he crawled out and climbed up onto my knees. It was the last flight of the tour and if the flight attendants found out about their extra passenger, it wouldn't really matter. The worst they could do would be to escort Tabasco off the plane. Come to think of it, that wouldn't be too bad an idea. After two weeks of travelling and collecting more baggage, I could have used some help.

Tabasco fell asleep and I lay back to do what I hadn't time to do on the trip—read my book.

"I wonder what it's like to have a raccoon in one's parka?" asked my fellow passenger, who had noticed the book but not its live subject. "Where do you think she really keeps it?"

"On my lap," I grinned.

He looked down. "You're kidding, right?"

"No," I said innocently. "Look again."

Once again, he glanced down. Then he laughed. "Okay. It's stuffed."

I tickled Tabasco under the chin. His eyes opened and he stretched out lazily.

Tabasco had big, bright, beady eyes and thick, shiny fur. The man stared at him. "My God! I don't believe it!" he said.

In his short life, Tabasco had amazed a lot of people. He had charmed adults and children alike. He had appealed to their need to touch something wild.

CHAPTER THREE

THERE'S A RACCOON IN MY APARTMENT

"Well, how did the macaroon make out?" Dad asked anxiously when Tabasco and I got back to the apartment.

"No worries, mate," I said breezily. Mom and Dad would be returning to Australia soon and I wanted their last few days with me to be relaxed. Well, as relaxed as possible considering I lived with a raccoon.

Fortunately, Tabasco still spent most of his time between feedings cuddled up to his toque in a large cardboard box. Maybe it was jet lag or maybe it was because he was still only a month-old baby, but he seemed quite content to sleep in my office beside my desk or my bed. If we left him alone in the apartment I put his box in the bathroom. I figured that it was easier to clean up a bathroom after a raccoon than any other room in a house. Besides, Tabasco was used to bathrooms, the best ones in the country.

No longer did I have to rub his tummy and backside as a mother raccoon would, to stimulate urination and defecation. Toilet training had begun, much to the relief of my patient parents. Tabasco now climbed out of his box den and "went" in a corner on papers—most of the time. "Animals in the house are not my cup of tea," said my mother resignedly as she watched where she walked.

Now that we were back home I had more time to watch Tabasco grow. He had increased his milk intake to four ounces at each feeding. With four canine teeth, six incisors on the bottom and four on top, he had begun to bite the nipple instead of sucking it. "I'm glad we'll be gone by the time he starts on us," said Dad wryly, running a hand over his bald head.

Instead of going back to sleep after each feed, Tabasco now played. At first he just played by himself, lying on his back tugging his toes or chasing his tail. Then he played with the box, the towel and the toque. Soon he ventured farther afield, instinctively climbing out of the box and up our legs. Unfortunately, polyester pants and skirts were the fashion at the time and his sharp little claws left unsightly pulls all over our clothes to mark each ascent.

Once on top of our shoulders, he stretched up to paw our heads, feeling for the nooks and crannies of our faces, poking his sensitive black suede fingers into our noses, our ears, our mouths. "You should call him Goesinta because he goes into everything," suggested one of the neighbourhood kids.

Dad had other names when the raccoon latched onto the last of the grey hairs that lapped across his shiny dome or when "the little monster" bit and tugged with teeth and claws at his unprotected ears. The most printable of them was the Rackety Macaroon because he made such a racket. But to be fair, when Dad was raked across his bald head by Tabasco's claws, he made just as much noise as the raccoon. Tabasco purred when he was content, squeaked when he greeted a friend, churred and chittered when he went exploring, growled when he acted angry or faced a foe, but positively shrieked when in a strange place like the hall outside the apartment. Fortunately, my neighbours worked and were away much of the time. Or else they were deaf. Rarely did I meet them on the stairs but Mom always had her apology ready.

Tabasco also shrieked when he heard a strange sound. In one of his after-dinner play flurries, he'd scamper amid the newspapers spread on the floor of the bathroom, snatch and crumple it into balls and, when the crackling paper "talked back," go into defence mode. He'd take a step backwards, quickly draw in his breath, hiss and, bristling his fur like a prickly porcupine, SHRIEK. Strangely, in these early weeks, he was scared of water. At bathtime he didn't know whether to bite the hand that was pulling him down into it or use it as a lever to get himself out of it. While he was deciding he SHRIEKED.

Living in a no-dog, no-cat apartment, we were always conscious of the landlady. Fortunately, she lived in a different building so couldn't hear Tabasco's screeches. Unfortunately, her window overlooked my spot in the parking lot. My strategy to keep Tabasco hidden was to bundle him up in a brown paper bag that I put in the back of the car before I got into the driver's seat. When I returned to the parking lot I did things in reverse. To curious eyes staring down from the apartments above, Tabasco was just a bag of groceries. At least, that's what I hoped.

As Tabasco's play periods grew longer, so did his need to explore. He followed feet. A roly-poly little fluffball, he bounced along, back and forth, up and down, swaying from side to side, dancing more than walking. I was enchanted. Although they wouldn't admit it, so were Mom and Dad—until Tabasco walked into Mom's macramé. He lay on his back, hands and feet working busily in the air, tying more knots in a few minutes than she had in the previous weeks of her crafts course.

"Lynette! Ted! Get that creature out of my yarn. It's the final night of my course tonight and he's wrecking my plant holder. Oh, no! Now he's found my knitting."

The instructor didn't get a chance to show her approval but Tabasco did. He loved Mom's macramé. He pranced around the pile of yarn and wool like a boxer testing his punches, then finding it didn't fight back, he plunged right into the fray. He snatched and tugged, he bit and shook and tore, till pieces of plant hanger and skeins of unravelled sweater were pulled down from the coffee table, the chesterfield and the chair, and littered the living room floor.

Then, suddenly aware of danger looming above in the form of Mom, Dad and me, he hissed, arched his back into a skunk-like stripe, opened and shut his mouth on a pile of wool and, with strands trailing behind, scampered with it down the corridor to the security of his box in the bathroom. I snipped him out of the woollen coat he was making for himself and discreetly closed the door.

"I'll kill him," Mom wailed, gathering up what was left of her murdered macramé. "Jan will never be able to stand it. You will have to get rid of that raccoon when she comes."

Fortunately for my parents' nerves, they flew back to Australia the following week, and fortunately for me, I had six weeks to get Tabasco ready for the arrival of my sister Jan. By then, I would have finished my summer semester at university, and Jan, Tabasco and I would be able to leave the city to explore the great outdoors. At least, that was what I hoped.

"Tabasco!" I told the raccoon sternly, staring into his cheeky face and bright beady eyes. "You'll have to smarten up. You've got to learn to eat stuff other than milk, you've got to climb and swim and hike, and PLEASE help me keep this apartment tidy. My sister's coming. Okay?"

As I was doing a directed study program at university rather than classroom work, I had to go to school only once or twice a week. Tabasco and I spent the rest of the time alone in the apartment. He was always on his best behaviour when there were no other adults around to distract him or make him jealous.

Some nights he slept beside me on the pillow with his tail tucked under my chin. When his furry closeness tickled me or my nighttime thrashing disturbed him, I carried him off to his box in the bathroom and tried to close my ears to his churring entreaties. When I opened the door in the morning the bathroom usually had remained undisturbed and he greeted me sleepily with a yawn and a stretch. He'd follow me to the kitchen and continue sleeping curled up on my feet like a cinnamon bun. Feeling obliged not to wake him, I'd find myself standing at the sink keeping one foot in place while I leaned backwards on the other foot, reaching for dishes in a cupboard or bending sideways to put a pot on the stove.

Coffee and muffin in hand, and with a live raccoon-fur slipper on foot, I'd then hobble to my office. Each time the living room phone rang or I'd need another cup of coffee or I wanted to pick up the mail, I would try to sneak away but he always knew. He'd sense my departure, wake up instantly and take off like a shot to look for me in the other rooms. Then back he'd go to the office to sleep on my foot, my lap or the typewriter cover stored in the dark den under my desk.

If he woke at all, he'd purr a few notes of recognition, yawn and, with eyes still closed, start sucking on my finger. Then he'd turn over to lie on his back and start grooming by nibbling his tummy and the inside of his legs. Awake but not yet ready to attack the day, he'd sniff under any papers within reaching distance, poke his nose and fingers into the closest drawers, play feelies with my watch, pull gently at my hair. To be touched by the soft, sensitive hands of a raccoon is a privilege and a delight. Slowly, delicately yet purposefully, he would squeeze open my mouth, force my lips apart, then probe and poke and prod inside.

But then there were mornings when an incessant high-pitched shriek sent me scurrying to the bathroom and I opened the door on disaster. One day, I found Tabasco had tugged the toilet roll from its holder, looped it around the pedestal, and now that he could stand up on his hind legs to reach the seat, plopped what was left of the roll into the bowl. He'd tipped over the garbage can and spread hair, tissues and used tubes of cream and toothpaste over a soggy floor. He'd opened the cupboards and turfed out towels, boxes, bottles. He'd torn up the carpet, luckily mine, not the landlady's.

"Tabasco, you're rotten," I scolded, kneeling down to pick up the mess. With a purr and a pleased squeak to be with me again, he reached up to touch my face. I just couldn't stay mad.

After the bathroom incident, nothing in the apartment was safe. True to his nickname, Goesinta would go into everything: cans and boxes in the bathroom, pots and jars in the kitchen, drawers and cupboards in the living room. He regularly burgled purses and pockets. (No wonder raccoons are often called Bandit.) In those days before personal computers, I'd come back to the office to find a warm furry body prowling my typewriter, sticking the keys together, pulling out reams of ribbon and plugging the spaces with erasers, paper clips and thumbtacks.

And always, while his hands and feet were digging, his eyes remained riveted on the far horizon and his face said innocently, "Who, me?" One of the most disconcerting habits raccoons have is staring into space absentmind-edly while their hands are busily ferreting around the bottom of a cookie jar, a goldfish bowl, a purse, down your neck or any number of other off-limits places. So keen is their sense of touch that raccoons seem to see with their hands. They don't have to look at what they're getting into.

Raccoons make good vacuum cleaners. Their busy little paws are always feeling around, behind and under things. Tabasco often brought dust into the open— usually, to my embarrassment, as visitors were walking through the door.

Raccoons also make good detectives. They have the habit of unearthing the smallest things. If I've lost things to raccoons I've also had help finding them again. Tabasco collected what interested him and cached them in his hidey-hole under the chesterfield. He immediately noticed anything new. If I wore a new hairband or pair of earrings, Tabasco homed in on them instantly and climbed on top of my head to investigate. My only problem was that if he lost his balance he grabbed great gobs of my skin to regain it.

As part of my strategy to raccoon-proof the apartment, I made sure anything breakable was placed above his reach. But as his climbing ability improved and his reach extended, I had to keep moving the breakables higher. Tabasco kept tabs on their progress.

By mid-July, when he was about two months old, I took advantage of a raccoon's natural curiosity, its love to touch and its eventual love of water to wean Tabasco from his milk bottle.

He had now grown big enough to haul himself into the bathtub by means of a rubber mat draped over the side. (Although he climbed instinctively he had difficulty climbing on slippery surfaces.) He often followed me into the shower. The noise of the taps turning on sent him slippering to the end of the tub where he sat chasing the spray and catching drips. It was the sound he feared, not the water.

Many people think that a raccoon washes its food. It is often seen scratching around underwater with its hands and *Procyon lotor*, the Latin name scientists know it by, means "the washing dog." The French call it *raton laveur*, "the washing rat." The Germans call it *waschbär*, "the washing bear."

Although some scientists think that raccoons use water to remove secretions certain amphibians give off from their skin, raccoons have a reputation for cleanliness that they really don't deserve. Most experiments show that raccoons douse clean foods in water just as often as dirty foods. And much of their food is found near water, or in water, anyway.

What really happens is that raccoons have an incredible sense of touch and simply like feeling things. They instinctively roll their food between their sensitive front paws to sort out which food is which. They dip food in water only if water is available. One scientist discovered recently that raccoons in captivity seem to wash the food they are given as a way of recreating the washing habit of wild raccoons. Others say that raccoons in captivity appear to wash their food out of boredom. Perhaps a raccoon's sense of touch is stronger underwater. Perhaps only the raccoon knows.

Whatever the reason, I tried to entice Tabasco into

eating solids by appealing to his natural instincts. Besides, putting his food dish in the bathtub meant it was easier to clean up any mess. I filled the tub with an inch or two of water and put in his milk dish. As he padded gingerly around the bottom I threw in a smorgasbord of solid foods: peanuts, shrimp, sardines, grapes, pieces of apple, carrot and celery. I threw in eggs. Raccoons, so every farmer tells me, adore eggs.

Tabasco thought we were playing a game. He'd grasp a grape, plop it into his floating milk dish, slosh it around with his hands, lose it, chase it—do everything with it except eat it. He had always liked bright, shiny things. He'd roll an egg from one end of the tub to the other or pick it up with his teeth. Amazingly, he didn't break it—or eat it.

"This stuff's good for you," I kept telling Tabasco.

But he didn't take any notice. He got used to the water but he nudged every nutritious tidbit out of the way till he had lapped up his milk. To Tabasco, solid foods were still playthings.

"Well, at least playing with food now should teach you how to catch it in the wild later," I sighed. "But you'd better hurry up, you little ruffian, and start eating properly. I'm still at school, you're breaking my budget and Jan is coming soon."

By the time Tabasco was three months old he had lost his baby face and he had all his teeth so there was no excuse for him to drink milk. To hurry up the weaning process before Jan came, I gave in and tempted him with something that I knew all raccoon babies—perhaps all babies—liked: something sweet. Sugar might not be healthy but it is popular. Even while he was still on the milk bottle, Tabasco's busy little fingers would filch sugary cough lollies or throat lozenges out of their packets and he'd try to chew them.

I put Apple Jacks—a sugary breakfast cereal that you still see occasionally in the supermarket—into the tub. As I expected, he dived into the water with all four feet as if to play, bit into those sugary crunchies and became an Apple Jacks fan forever. As long as I coated food with a sprinkling of sugar or Apple Jacks he would eat anything.

THERE'S A RACCOON IN MY NEIGHBOURHOOD

One day in August, Tabasco flatly refused to have anything more to do with milk. He was weaned at last.

"Well, you little rascal, I guess we'd better go shopping and discover some of your favourite things," I announced one Saturday morning.

After peeking into the corridor and listening over the banisters to make sure nobody was looking, I tucked Tabasco under my arm to make him look like the garbage and started down our three flights of stairs. Carrying him saved time. Although he could go upstairs very well he had difficulty coming down and turning corners. When my feet disappeared around the bend of each landing he'd think himself lost and scuttle back upstairs again. He'd always go up in an emergency.

Travelling was simpler on level ground. To get to the shopping mall we had to walk along Hastings Street for three blocks. At first I carried him on my head like a live raccoon hat with his tail curled around my neck and his hands hanging on to my ears. It was one of his favourite positions because he could reach out to touch whatever attracted his curiosity. It was not my favourite position because if he wriggled around too much and lost balance his claws dug blood from my bone. As long as he kept close, following my feet was a much better method to get to the store. But if there were too many feet he got confused and started following anybody's.

I continued walking as if there was nothing unusual about my headgear or the fact that a raccoon was scampering behind. People stared, fascinated. They thought Tabasco was trained. They didn't realize he was doing what comes naturally. Raccoon kits in the wild follow their mother for survival.

Children often stopped us and asked excited questions. "Is that really a raccoon on your head?" "Did you know there's a raccoon running along behind you?"

"A raccoon?" I'd echo in surprise. Sometimes I'd say, "It's stuffed," or "It's working on batteries." Some kids would laugh. Others would stand open-mouthed in wonder. Mothers tried to scoot Tabasco off the footpath. That made him prance towards the road. As cars swerved and screeched around him, I dodged people and vehicles to snatch him out of harm's way.

We arrived at the post office first. The sign on the door said NO ANIMALS ALLOWED INSIDE. HEALTH REGULATIONS.

A few feet away, an earnest little boy of about eleven was waiting for a bus. "Would you mind hanging on to this while I pop inside to get some stamps?" I asked sweetly, putting Tabasco into his startled arms before he could say no.

"What'll I do when the bus comes?" he managed to say when he realized what was happening.

"Just shout and I'll come right away."

Inside there was a long lineup at the stamp wicket. I couldn't use "My raccoon is waiting for me at the bus stop" as an excuse to barge ahead. Nobody would believe me. I glanced outside. My raccoon-sitter was standing with his arms locked, too scared to move but totally awestruck. Tabasco was used to being passed around by people and he was always more gentle with children than adults. He stayed where he was put.

And then I saw the bus. Half a dozen customers were still waiting in line ahead of me. I had no choice. I raced outside to the street. "Thanks," I said, as if babysitting raccoons at bus stops was something that happened every day. I grabbed Tabasco and the boy boarded his bus. I grinned. What would he tell his parents that night?

Disregarding the NO ANIMALS sign, I rejoined the lineup in the post office. To my surprise, instead of asking me to leave, everybody clustered around to ask questions, even the postmistress.

"Where did you get him?"

"Where do you keep him?"

"What's his name?"

I would have stayed longer but it was difficult to lick stamps and answer questions with a raccoon trying to clamber down from my head. Tabasco recognized an office when he saw one. All those books, pens and pencils, paper clips, even a typewriter. All those new but familiar things. We left.

There was another NO ANIMALS sign on the door of the supermarket but with nobody outside waiting to catch a bus and the thought of Tabasco let loose on all the goodies in a grocery store, I decided to go back to the apartment for the car.

This time a little girl in pigtails and glasses followed us home and there was no way we could get away from her. She was as persistent as a raccoon. I pretended Tabasco didn't belong to me and I acted dumb as she asked a stream of questions. But she was determined.

"Is this where you live? I live next door. Who's your landlady?"

"I don't really know," I mumbled hastily as soon as we got to the door of our apartment block. "Goodbye. I have to meet someone."

I dashed up the stairs two at a time and she followed as fast as her fat little legs could run. Tabasco, hearing her footsteps chasing him from behind and seeing mine fleeing away from him in front, was spurred on to his best upstairs speed yet. "Scoot, coon," I hissed, as I scuttled around in my purse for the key to our apartment. We ducked inside just in time to lean backwards against the door and hear her knocking on my neighbour's door, a neighbour who was not at home on Saturdays.

I didn't dare go out shopping again till a couple of days later. This time I took the car. Just as I was depositing Tabasco in the back of the station wagon and hoping the landlady couldn't see the contents of my brown paper bag, the same little girl's shrill voice rang out from the top window of the neighbouring building. "Are you taking your coon for a walk again?"

I quickly dived for the driver's seat and drove off.

There weren't too many people around at the shopping mall. It was a hot day and many people had probably gone to the beach. I had to leave the car windows open to give Tabasco enough fresh air but I couldn't leave too big a slit. Somebody might try to pull him out or he might try to get out himself.

Joe, the produce manager, was delighted to fill a bag of fruits and vegetables for a raccoon. "We end up throwing most of this stuff out. You say he likes grapes and cherries. Here, try him on avocados, peaches and nectarines. And I bet he likes watermelon."

A few minutes later I was perusing the cat and dog food wondering which brand Tabasco might prefer when the manager's voice came over the loudspeaker system. "You may not believe this, shoppers, but will the owner of a red Mazda station wagon please get her pet raccoon? He's prowling the parking lot."

I left my groceries in the cart and dashed back to the car. The windows were all down. Had Tabasco done that? Raccoons can turn on taps and open refrigerator doors but surely he was still too young and uncoordinated to wind down windows. Had someone in the jostle of people around the car done it? Perhaps someone tried to steal him? The brown paper bag on the driver's seat wasn't the one Tabasco had arrived in.

"Wanna find your raccoon?" said somebody behind me. "He's on his way to the liquor store."

I caught up to Tabasco as he was dancing through the door. "Sorry, sir, this raccoon is underage!"

The man coming out with an armful of bags grinned. "I'm the one who should be sorry," he said apologetically. "I almost stepped on him."

Joe was waiting at the station wagon with Tabasco's goodies and a huge dish of water. "I thought he'd be thirsty." Far from it. Tabasco didn't wet his lips but he sure wet the back seat of the car. He dabbled and danced and dived in the water dish, soaking everything in sight while his ever-expanding audience squealed in delight. Tabasco was beginning to be a ham.

It was hot every day and I hated studying indoors when the weather was fine. I found lots of excuses to leave the apartment. Everywhere I went Tabasco went too. "You were born in the city so you may as well get used to the city," I told him.

Early on I thought I should try him on a leash. The lady behind the counter was charmed to have a raccoon come into her pet store. "Go and fetch him a cookie," she tittered in delight to her daughter. She was not so charmed a few moments later when Tabasco bit her as she struggled to contain his squirming body between the elastic straps of a cat harness. Trouble is, raccoons are not cats—or dogs. Tabasco's front paws were the problem. They didn't stay down like a cat's or a dog's. They were hands, always poking up through the straps and trying to remove them—which they did.

"Why don't you try a collar?" the lady suggested, trying to contain her impatience as well as the raccoon.

"No, I had one once for another raccoon and he got his collar caught in the branches when he climbed trees."

Raccoons are tremendously strong in relation to their size. They can beat up dogs much bigger than themselves. The pet store lady was no match for a baby raccoon determined to get out of a flimsy cat harness. Tabasco wriggled and squirmed and clawed—and bit.

"Ouch! He got me, he's a monster," she shrieked, pulling her hands away from their stranglehold on her customer and wiping up the blood.

"Let's try a leather one," I said soothingly, "and I'll bribe him with sugar."

Her daughter got another cookie and by shoving it into Tabasco's mouth to divert his teeth from our flesh, I finally got him into the harness. It was strong but way too big.

"It needs more holes but I don't have anything to do them with here," the pet store owner said hastily, as if her customer was not quite so welcome now.

"That's okay, I'll do it at home," I said, handing her fifteen dollars for a harness and leash that both Tabasco and I knew we would probably never use.

After that, Tabasco stayed so close to my feet that I sometimes tripped over him. He was determined not to wear *that thing* again.

Tabasco loved to visit schools. Except for hissing and growling at a stuffed seal in a sleeping bag that students of Haney School had made after reading one of my books, Tabasco was on his best behaviour with children. He didn't have to demand their attention as with some adults; he got it immediately. In fact, they spoiled him rotten. He was reverently passed around from one child to another. He was given a bowl of milk and allowed to tramp milky footprints everywhere. He could pry into desks, roam around tables, throw books off shelves, pull the beards and ears of teachers—and get away with it. He could do things elsewhere that I would not tolerate at home.

And he loved it. Raccoons are known for their intelligence. Tabasco often tested my patience on purpose. At home he was toilet trained to a box of newspapers or paper towels in a corner, things that are easily obtainable anywhere. At Haney, he made straight for his toilet box and, just as I was pointing out how well he was trained, he left his corner, walked over to me and messed all down my pants as I was picking him up. He enjoyed the wild guffaws of the twenty-five children in his audience. In fact, applause sent this raccoon into an actor's heaven. He made his exit to the car in a wild dance of excitement.

On his first day at my big school, Simon Fraser University, he was nervous like any new student. He kept so close to my heels on the way to the library from the parking lot that I trod on him twice. And he conked himself on the head when he tried to dive through a door without waiting for it to be opened. He almost broke the glass.

He did break up two groups of sunbathing students reading on the lawn. Their school work couldn't compete with a scampering raccoon. By the time we got to the ornamental pool, Tabasco had a new bevy of admirers. But pride goes before a fall. Just as he was posing for one of the student's cameras at the edge of the pool, the photographer stepped forward for a portrait shot, the raccoon stepped backward—and fell into the water. Instead of chasing the goldfish, as he would probably learn to do later, he clambered out immediately, turned around and gave a long hard look at the water. He reached forward cautiously with one paw, thrust his nose down to touch the silvery surface and, to my surprise, fell in again. I had to fish him out. The students cheered and went back to their books.

A raccoon's bulging, round, shiny eyes are far better adapted for night than daytime vision. Their pupils open wide to let in maximum light, the cornea covering their lenses is large and cone-shaped, and a special layer of cells behind the retina increases the raccoon's ability to see in low light. Perhaps Tabasco fell into the pool because he was more used to seeing in the dark den under my desk. Perhaps his curious nose led him further than his brains. Perhaps he caught sight of his reflection and got scared of the strange raccoon as had happened before in the bathroom mirror. Perhaps he just needed a broader experience with water than the apartment bathroom—which was not much use anyway as he invariably pulled the plug every time I filled the tub.

From then on, Tabasco and I spent mornings in the apartment or at school and afternoons around water: a pool, an inlet, a creek, a river or a lake.

So as not to bump into the landlady or the little girl who'd followed us home from the store, most days

I carried Tabasco downstairs and across busy Hastings Street to a park with tennis courts, climbing equipment and a wading pool. In the early afternoon we usually had the park to ourselves. Tabasco would get his exercise by running after the tennis balls that I missed batting against the wall. After school, children would take him on their laps for rides down the slide until he got the confidence to come down by himself.

The shiny steel bars of the climbing equipment posed a special challenge for Tabasco. He was just getting used to the stairs. He hadn't yet encountered trees. He'd grip the slippery surface of the climbing bars with all four feet and belly scrape along. Sometimes, he'd teeter-totter, lose his balance and slide into an upside down position, but the children were there with helping hands to make sure he didn't fall. As usual, coming down was more difficult. He could either back down or descend headfirst. A raccoon's claws are sharp and curved to help them dig into the rough bark of a tree but they are not much help gripping a slippery pipe.

The wading pool was only a foot deep, an ideal place to begin swimming lessons. It didn't take Tabasco long to learn. As soon as he got the confidence to try he did it instinctively. Survival taught him the strokes. Practice made him perfect. The neighbourhood children hovered over him anxiously as he dabbled in to his elbows then launched himself across to the other side. He looked like a half-submerged pincushion as he paddled with fingers splayed out in front, tail plumed out behind, pointed ears and shiny black nose sticking up out of the water and stiff white whiskers stretched forward around his muzzle.

Soon Tabasco was ready to try the ocean.

Motorists roaring along Hastings Street in rush hour traffic probably never realized how close they were to a quiet beach on Burrard Inlet. It took Tabasco and me only a few minutes to cross the park, walk down a bush trail to the railway line and then scramble down the bank to the water. It was an inviting area, especially when the tide was out, despite the sign that said SEWER OUTFALL 350 FEET. Perhaps it was the sewer outfall that made the intertidal area so productive.

Raccoons forage instinctively. Still making sure he kept close to my feet, Tabasco pranced in and out of pools of water, playing feelies with strands of yellowy brown seaweed. He turned over pebbles and scraped off the barnacles. He crunched limpets and mussels. At first I had to lever them off the rocks for him but later he did it himself.

Little hermit crabs scurried away and he gave chase but he couldn't catch them. I grabbed them myself and popped them into a jar. In true Goesinta fashion he couldn't resist reaching inside and taking them out. He'd bat them around, toss them into the air, rush in and catch them—over and over again. He was playing a game, but it was a game that wild raccoons need to play for survival. He winced when one of the crab's pincers pinched his sensitive paw.

"Guess you'll have to learn how to hold down those pincers when you start getting bigger crabs, Tabasco," I smiled sympathetically.

"Do you want some of ours?"

I looked up to see two boys standing beside us with a whole bucket of crabs in their hands.

"If you go on the dock you can get real big ones," said the taller of the two teenagers.

"Can we play with your raccoon? We'll be very careful," asked the one with glasses.

"Well, I don't think he's going to get very far away from me till he's used to you but why don't you play with him around here. It'll give me a chance to study."

There were two docks leading out from the beach, one that the locals used for fishing and crabbing at high tide, and the other with a little shed at the end used by boom men when they were sorting logs. On this day the tide was very low and exposed enough beach area that you could walk out as far as the huge rafts of logs.

"Can Tabasco go with us to the log boom?" asked Paul, the younger of the two brothers. "We drop our traps over the side of the logs and it just takes ten minutes or so to get some real good ones."

For the next hour while I sat on a rock with my book, Danny and Paul took Tabasco for a stroll out to the logs and taught him how to catch crabs. Every now and then, Tabasco looked up and made his little churring sound to keep contact with me.

"Can we take Tabasco and show our dad?" asked Danny. "He's fishing from the dock."

"Sure, let's go together."

I liked the two boys immediately. They were polite, respectful, fascinated with Tabasco and really interested in his education. So was their dad. Lino, an Italian plumber, lived alone with his two sons in a large house on the other side of Burnaby Mountain, not far from Simon Fraser University.

"Why don't you bring Tabasco and have supper with us tonight?" he asked.

"Yes, Dad makes great gnocchi and ravioli," put in Paul excitedly. "And Tabasco can walk in the woods and swim in our neighbour's pool."

"And we can take him crayfishing in the creek," added Danny enthusiastically.

"Perhaps he'd like to hike around Burnaby Lake," Lino suggested.

And so Lino, Danny and Paul became Tabasco's official babysitters. The Gonzato family kept their house so immaculate I didn't dare let the raccoon inside but there were plenty of things to interest him outside. He perfected his swimming techniques in the neighbour's pool, which Paul was allowed to use in exchange for keeping it clean. Tabasco practised coming down tree trunks in the woods along the back fence, forwards AND backwards. He pirouetted among the water lilies on Burnaby Lake and scattered the ducks.

But most of all he learned to eat crabs and fish and crayfish.

At first he just played with them like a hyperactive child with a short attention span. Then one day at the sewer outfall beach where we'd met, Paul caught a monster Dungeness crab with mussel bait. "Here, Tabasco, catch," he called, throwing the crab in front of the raccoon.

Tabasco latched on to one of the legs, remembered those pincers could bite so wisely nipped it off at the thigh joint, then closed his mouth over the carapace. He bit a hole in the crab's shell. A hole! Oh, joy for a raccoon. In he dug with curled fingers and scooped out the juicy meat. Shuck, shuck, shuck. He slurped noisily. His mouth clacked open and shut in rhythmic beats of satisfaction. By the time he had finished he'd eaten that crab shell and all.

"How can he digest that hard stuff?" asked Danny, more as a statement of amazement than a question.

Tabasco's shiny fur and well-formed black droppings showed that he did.

Adapting Tabasco to a wild diet was becoming a round-the-clock routine. We went crayfishing after dark in Burnaby Creek. Paul took off his shoes and socks and waded through the cold water with a net on the end of a long pole. Danny scouted the deepest holes and turned over rocks. Lino and I shivered behind, carrying the lights. Tabasco lollygagged around us, poked his nose into anything that attracted his attention, climbed the trees overhanging the creek—and waited for handouts. Why try if somebody else is willing to do the work, I bet he was thinking.

"Lazy!" I admonished. "You're better equipped for cold water than we are, Tabasco. You've got fur, we've got bare legs." The raccoon paid no attention.

"I've got one," Paul yelled. "I need more light."

Like a shot, Tabasco scurried down a nearby sapling to be the first on the scene. He knew exactly what he wanted and how to get it. Before any of us registered what was happening, he had grabbed the crayfish out of Paul's hands and splashed through the shallow water with it to the bank.

Lino made a move to take it from him so I could get a photograph but Tabasco was determined not to let go, not even for a moment. He hissed, bristled and backed up against the bank, the crayfish dangling from his jaws. While we went back to the hole for more, he pinioned the pincers against the pebbles, cracked open the flipping tail and started to crunch.

Paul soon got another. Again Tabasco whipped in to pick it up. This time, Paul held it up above the raccoon's head so I could get a picture. Undaunted, Tabasco reached up on his hind legs, leaped and snatched the crayfish out of the air.

"Boy, Tabasco, you could play soccer," Lino said admiringly.

Two handouts were enough for one night. We caught two more for the freezer and then went home. Next time, Tabasco would have to catch the crayfish himself.

Although Lino, Danny and Paul were Tabasco's chief friends and sole babysitters, the raccoon had plenty of other companions. We often visited Ivy, one of my student friends from university who had a big house and swimming pool in a woodsy area of North Vancouver. She also had a Persian cat and a big Doberman dog.

Tabasco hadn't yet had much to do with other animals. The few dogs he'd met on the beach or at the shopping mall usually ran away when they saw him coming. But

Ivy's animals were very independent. They were used to raccoons. This time, it was Tabasco who wanted to run away. But he was a plucky little animal and perhaps had more bravado than brains. Front paws planted firmly and wide apart in front of him, snout down, perky nose up, bristling rump held high in the air, tail slashing from side to side—he stood his ground and dared either the cat or the dog to come near him.

One day, Mom and Dad sent me a box of crayfish from Down Under. They're the saltwater kind with fat tails but no pincers and are trapped on the reefs of Rottnest Island where my parents live on a boat. Except for their lack of pincers, Aussie crayfish are just like North American lobsters. "Give one to Tabasco and see how he likes it compared to the kind he catches in Burnaby Creek," wrote my Dad in an accompanying note.

Tabasco didn't appreciate the fine gastronomic differences between freshwater crayfish and lobster, which was just as well as I love Aussie crayfish so much. I thought I'd invite our friend Ernie to share them instead, at a picnic on Belcarra Beach on the other side of Burrard Inlet.

It was another unbelievably hot summer day and Tabasco made a few more friends on the way to the beach. The winding trail through the woods was crowded with people and their pets. Usually, Tabasco kept within voice contact and close to my feet. When challenged by a dog or cat he went into his "I am bigger than you" stance and hoped for the best. If he didn't think he had a chance of winning, he'd escape up a tree.

Today he bounced all over the place. He reached up salal bushes and tore off berries with both paws. He scratched around in the dirt for insects or worms. He chased a couple of teasing kids up a tree then disappeared over a bank. While I rescued the children and Ernie tried to calm their dad, people on the other side of the bank were trying to catch Tabasco. Unlike with children, it was difficult to train a raccoon not to talk to strangers.

"Let's skip this beach and find a quieter one," Ernie suggested. "Otherwise, Tabasco is going to get himself into more trouble."

Trouble was waiting just around the corner. We came out of the woods into a secluded cove and ran right into Sadie, a black and tan coonhound.

"Grab your raccoon," yelled Jo, a tall, tanned girl who was running towards us from a beach cottage. "My dogs'll make mincemeat out of it."

There wasn't one coon hunting dog but two. Up from behind Sadie came Luke, a bluetick hound who also had thousands of years of hunting the likes of Tabasco in his genes.

To my surprise, the raccoon was so busy turning over the pebbles on this new beach that he scarcely seemed to notice the two big hounds towering over him.

The dogs certainly noticed, though. This was one raccoon that didn't run. Tabasco didn't back up either. In fact, he turned around to face the hounds and slowly strode towards them.

We were all transfixed, Jo, Ernie, Sadie, Luke and me. None of the humans had the courage to intervene in what we all expected to be a bloodbath. The dogs' eyes bulged.

And then Tabasco charged. It was the dogs' turn to run—off to tell their littermates chasing deer in the bush the story of the strange raccoon now nipping at their heels. Tabasco returned triumphantly to the beach—alone.

"That's some spunky raccoon," Jo marvelled as she introduced herself. "A raccoon hounding my hounds!"

"What else does he do?" smiled the young man joining us from the cabin. "My name's Brian."

"You never know with Tabasco," I laughed.

But Tabasco did add some new skills to his repertoire that day. Brian and Ernie launched a log into the water and Tabasco, ever curious, swam out to it. He tried climbing aboard, but as it rolled over in the water he couldn't catch hold of its slippery surface and he kept falling back. Sympathetic to his plight, I picked him out of the water and set him astride the log.

As he started walking along it, the log started to roll and the more Tabasco walked, the more the log rolled. Within minutes, it looked as if the raccoon was twirling the log like a real log birler. Perhaps he had been watching the boom men on the logs by the sewer outfall back home where he got his crabs. Suddenly, he must have missed a beat. He and the log rolled together, both going the same way, and Tabasco did his first kayak roll.

His instincts told him to hang on. His tough little claws dug into the bark of the tree, and he closed his eyes, disappeared underwater and—miraculously it seemed to us—came up unharmed on the other side. He then and there decided against a career in log birling.

Later on, after a picnic on the beach shared with Ernie, Brian and Jo (her hounds didn't risk joining us), Tabasco tried a variation on following feet and followed Brian's canoe onto the water. Unlike the log, the canoe didn't roll and pull him under.

"I think you've had enough underwater work for one day, Tabasco," Brian said, helping the raccoon into the canoe. Once aboard, Tabasco shook the water out of his fur, groomed, then stood in the bow looking out to sea like a Viking warrior.

Ernie observed when we got home, "Tabasco sure adds spice to life." I told him about Mr. McIlhenny, who makes Tabasco sauce in Louisiana. He had read about Tabasco in a Montreal newspaper and wrote to ask if I had named my raccoon after his sauce. When I replied that I had, he sent me a dozen bottles of it.

A peppery character who added spice to life wherever he went—that was Tabasco. He was little but instantly noticed, just like his namesake, the sauce.

CHAPTER FIVE

THERE'S A RACCOON ON MY CAMPING TRIP

Tabasco was getting so used to visiting that he wasn't content to spend all day in the apartment sitting on my lap or sleeping at my feet. He got bored playing in the bathroom by himself.

"Okay, Tabasco, you can play in my office but I'm going to be busy. Jan is arriving in a few days and I've got to finish my university work. Then we can have fun."

But Tabasco wanted fun now. He tipped over the wastepaper basket a dozen times and I cleaned it up a dozen times till I realized that playing feelies with crumpled paper, muffin cups, stubby pencils and used pens could keep him occupied for hours. Pilfering my purse and spreading the contents over the floor kept him busy for another hour, even longer if he decided to take something to his chesterfield cache. Pulling down clothes from their hangers in the office closet filled in a few more minutes as did throwing books on the floor and tearing invoices off book packages.

After a day of sitting at a typewriter my legs feel like curdled jelly. I need exercise too. Tabasco would tempt me into playing with him by leaping onto my lap, clawing his way to my shoulder, pulling my hair, jumping down to the floor again and rolling over, inviting me to tickle his tummy.

I joined the game by running around the apartment on tiptoe, wondering what the tenants below thought of our patter. Space was limited so I wove as long a course as possible—trotting in and out of the bathroom, the bedroom, the office and around the kitchen and living room, sneaking behind the furniture and room dividers, playing peekaboo and jumping out at the raccoon as he made another flying leap into my arms.

Raccoons like the security of small, dark spaces, and Tabasco spent the longest time getting into my desk drawers. Despite his cramped position, he would squeeze himself between the narrow wooden compartments and play there all morning or afternoon. When I reached for an eraser I'd get a raccoon. And he was a natural at hide-and-seek. Tabasco would squeeze himself behind the refrigerator, between the stove and the counter or under the chesterfield. If I chased him he always chose those hiding places first, places I couldn't easily reach. Believe me, raccoons know how to smile.

Tabasco added variations to our game of hide-and-seek by flying onto tables, slithering down shiny countertops, vaulting onto shelves, pulling the phone off the hook and dragging rugs down the corridor. Often his finale was dashing to my desk, bounding onto the shelf above my typewriter and tipping the teapot onto the keys. If I had no time to rewrite a report I would have to add a note to the teacher at the end of a soggy page: "Sorry, but Tabasco did this."

These raccoon variations to our game were all against the rules. At each violation I became the umpire and yelled, "No!" The guilty player usually stopped immediately, then headed for the chesterfield where he played with his toys or lay on his back and languidly pulled out their stuffing.

The time had come to let Tabasco out on the balcony. It would give him more room to exercise with fewer rules and give my sister more room too when she came.

Tabasco knew that gulls, pigeons and starlings were his balcony neighbours. His ears stood to attention at each squawk or coo or chitter. He could see the birds through the window or patio doors but I hadn't let him meet them in person.

The birds would not want a resident raccoon living with them on the balcony so obviously some would have to vacate. My friend Jack from the Fish and Wildlife Branch came to take away the pigeons. The one-legged gull still flew onto the railing but he timed his visits for when no masked bandit was around. The starlings seemed safe because Tabasco couldn't climb smooth vertical walls—at least not yet. And the patio furniture was durable.

"Well, Tabasco," I told my roommate, "I don't think you can do much damage out here—except swing on my hanging baskets—and you wouldn't touch those, would you? Jan loves flowers."

Tabasco could do damage to himself, though, I thought anxiously as he hoisted himself up the balcony posts and tottered along the railing. Like any mother watching her child's first climb, I hovered alongside ready to snatch him into my arms at the first sign of danger. But a raccoon who could climb on trees, log booms and playground equipment, who could swim and slide and birl, who could tackle cats and dogs, felt right at home on the balcony. Almost immediately, he was balancing on two feet and stretching up to pull at the leaves of the plants in the hanging baskets. I was so amazed by his fearlessness and natural sense of balance that I ignored the threat to my plants.

From then on Tabasco spent hours on the balcony, stretched out along the railing looking up at the twittering starlings or down at the noisy traffic. As long as the raccoon saw me through my office window he was content to stay outside all day. And it was easier for me to get the apartment ready for Jan without him chasing the vacuum cleaner cord or pulling things out of cupboards as soon as I put them in.

"Don't you think you should bring your sister home from the airport to a raccoon-free apartment?" Ivy suggested a couple of days before Jan Day as we stood chest-deep in her pool, balancing one side of a big rubber tire while Tabasco balanced the other side. "At least for the first night till she gets over jet lag?" she added hastily, seeing the look of shock on my face at the very idea of going to the airport without my raccoon.

But the more I thought about it the better an idea it seemed. I loved my sister dearly but I wondered how she was going to cope with Tabasco's lifestyle, either in or out of the apartment.

My sister was always trying to appear cool, calm and collected. She looked and talked as if she were attending a garden party at Buckingham Palace. Unlike Tabasco, she liked to be just so and have everything in its place. Still, underneath her cool exterior, Jan had our family's sense of fun and I knew that would help her survive a month with Tabasco. Mom and Dad would surely have warned her about the trials and tribulations of living with a raccoon, especially in a third-floor apartment.

Nevertheless, I decided a babysitter might be a good idea, at least for the first day. Lino and the boys were delighted to look after the raccoon. While they pampered my little monster and prepared the basement for his accommodation, I freshened up by taking a quick dip in their pool.

"Thanks a lot, guys," I said as I towelled my hair. "We'll come and get Tabasco tomorrow." I had an idea. "We're doing a TV show tomorrow night at the CTV studios right by your place. You can be in the audience if you like. How about we go crayfishing first so he'll have some good stuff to eat?"

With arrangements made for the next day, I rushed off to the airport. It was sweltering but I was glad that Jan would have such fantastic weather on her first visit to Vancouver. I could just imagine her sitting in the window seat taking pictures of the city's beautiful mountain backdrop as the plane came in for its final approach. Soon we would be out in those mountains, hiking in that wilderness and camping in a tent with a raccoon. Summer school was over, but our summer was only about to begin!

The terminal doors slid open and, with temperatures soaring, out came my sister dressed for winter. She was wearing a fashionable three-piece fur-trimmed suit, a fur coat and a fur hat. She'd heard that Canada was a cold place so was wheeling a cart stacked high with suitcases full of clothes for a Canadian winter. And instead of looking into alpine lakes as the plane descended, she'd been in the washroom looking in a mirror at her makeup.

"Lynette! Where have you been? Your hair's wet. You're not wearing makeup. Did you forget to put your clothes on?" she said in between hugging and kissing. "But I'm glad to see you don't have that raccoon. Did you really expect me to live with it?"

"Well, not today," I said as cheerfully as I could. "No, you won't have any trouble today."

The landlady was waiting for us at the door when we arrived at the apartment. The owner of the building, a man, stood beside her. I had never seen him before. He looked like a very important person. And he had come to give me notice.

"We have been told you have a raccoon living here," the landlady said grimly. "People have been complaining that they are not allowed to have pets so why should you."

"Come inside and look for yourself," I said disarmingly. "There's no raccoon here."

Of course, there wasn't. Tabasco was at Lino's. We walked into an empty and immaculate apartment, everything neat and clean and in its place. Everybody was surprised, my sister most of all.

"I'm so sorry for disturbing you," the landlady apologized. "I was really expecting a mess but you keep your place better than the other tenants."

"Well, I try hard," I replied truthfully. One has to really try hard when one lives with a raccoon.

The landlady and the owner stood to leave. Jan looked terrified, as if she were embarking on a life of crime and would soon be deported.

"I really like having you as a tenant," the landlady continued at the door. "A quiet student, living alone, no late parties and you keep the place so neat. The tenants say you're a writer too."

Obviously, she hadn't read my books. Otherwise, she'd know that I had the habit of sharing my home with animals.

"Actually, I do have a raccoon and he is here sometimes," I said. Perhaps it was best that I tell her the whole truth—well, almost all of it. The pigeons and the starlings and the gull came in from the wild to live on my balcony so why not a raccoon? "I'm studying wildlife at university," I explained. "But my course has just ended and I'm away in the field for the next few months. I was thinking of giving up the apartment anyway."

"Oh, no, I want you to stay," the landlady said hastily. "I was just worried about the state of the place. I thought a raccoon would do terrible damage." The owner nodded in agreement. It was obvious that neither believed I could have had a raccoon for a roommate.

Jan could now rest in peace for a while. In fact, we had her welcome party without her. After thirty-six hours on planes and in airports, she put her things in my bedroom and slept there right through the next day till it was time to pick up Tabasco.

"Wake up," I announced cheerfully. "Get dressed. We're going on TV."

"Really?" She sat up in bed, immediately interested. "And what should I wear?"

"Well, we're going to a creek to catch crayfish first, so you should plan accordingly. I suggest rubber boots, hip waders and thick gloves. Surely, you've got something suitable in all that luggage."

I was joking. I remembered that my sister wouldn't even go crayfishing on my dad's boat Down Under till she had carefully applied several coats of makeup, arranged and rearranged her coiffure, experimented with the best way of wearing her scarf and placed her Christian Dior sunglasses for the most fashionable effect. "What do the crayfish care at five o'clock in the morning?" my father would sigh as he waited patiently in the dinghy till she'd dressed.

Jan was delighted by Lino, Danny and Paul but she declined to shake hands with the raccoon. Fur coats were acceptable but she didn't want any close encounter with the real thing. At least, she was determined to stave off that moment as long as possible.

"How do they keep their place so immaculate when

they babysit a raccoon?" she asked in surprise, as I changed into a pantsuit in Lino's bedroom after our crayfishing trip to the creek.

"With difficulty," I replied cheerfully. I didn't tell her that Tabasco had the habit of ripping out their insulation and tipping everything over as soon as they cleaned up.

She could see for herself that the family adored the raccoon. "Paul sleeps with Tabasco on the pillow beside him," Lino told her. "The raccoon is cute when he stands up to the table or looks at you over a window ledge and all you can see is his snout and beady eyes. Or when he crosses his paws on his chest like he's praying. He looks so bright-eyed and innocent."

"Really?" Jan said politely though she looked disbelieving.

She was even less believing after the TV taping. "I went all dolled up in my furs," she wrote in a letter to our parents. "We arrived at the studios in a limousine with a uniformed chauffeur. The red carpet was rolled out. People were running around giving us the star treatment. I felt like a Hollywood movie star. I knew I could only be in America. Then that rotten sister of mine made me walk in CARRYING A BUCKET!"

She was thrilled that we got our own dressing room—and very put out when I put her to work keeping Tabasco out of the hundreds of tubes of makeup while they did me up. She had the best seat, right in front, in full view of the famous movie stars who'd been flown up from Hollywood to be guests on the show. Her pride that her own sister had a place among them suffered a terrible turn when Tabasco fled the set and I went after him—while the cameras were rolling. She watched in horror as Tabasco dismantled a flower arrangement, got bits of crayfish everywhere and altogether took over the show. "Kids were lying on the floor in giggles, they thought it was so funny. I was so embarrassed I could have crawled under the seat," she wrote.

"It's just when he's out with a lot of people that he wants to show off," I assured my sister after the show. "He's really quite all right when he's at home. You'll see."

Jan looked apprehensive as I sneaked the raccoon up the stairs. We walked inside. Before I could grab him, Tabasco flew past me, made straight for the macramé hanging basket that Mom had made for me, pulled himself up and started to swing on it like a pendulum. It fell to the floor, shattering the beautiful plant pot and spreading sand and water on the carpet.

"Don't worry," I babbled as I cleaned up the mess. "Tabasco will be no trouble when we get out into the Rockies. I've got the camping equipment all ready—the tent, the sleeping bags, the stove, the dried food, packsacks. You can go over the list with me and see if I've forgotten anything."

Jan's face became pale despite her makeup.

"Rockies? If I wanted to see rocks I would have stayed in Australia. I want to visit shopping malls, hotels and restaurants. I want to look at cars and clothes and nice homes. Do you really mean you want me to sleep in a tent? I have never gone camping in my life, especially not with a coon, a loony coon at that. And I wouldn't be seen dead in camping clothes. Lynette, you're crazy! Mom and Dad were right!"

I stopped her long enough to explain that the rocks in the Rockies were covered with green forests, snow-capped mountain peaks and beautiful lakes and streams. And that if she couldn't stand it in a tent we could perhaps stay at Château Lake Louise or the Banff Springs Hotel. She brightened up at the mention of the words "château" and "hotel."

I tried to get her used to the wilderness by exploring little pockets of wilderness and wildlife in the city. We started with Stanley Park. Tabasco kept close to our feet as we joined other hikers for a walk around the seawall. Every now and then we had to stop and explain to people that no, he hadn't escaped from the zoo, and no, he wasn't a trained circus animal and yes, he was real and yes, he would bite if you screamed or stopped him from doing what he wanted to do, and yes, he was cute. People seemed to be sincerely interested in learning about Tabasco and I didn't mind how many times we stopped to answer their questions. Of course, they all wanted to touch him and, as long as they didn't tease, the raccoon didn't mind at all. I think my sister was beginning to see Tabasco in a different light.

One of our favourite pockets of wilderness close to the apartment was Sasamat Lake. Jan and I would walk along the beach with Tabasco happily scampering behind. On hot days the beach was always crowded but it got even more crowded when Tabasco romped along. He was no respecter of personal space. He walked over everyone and everything. He bounced over blankets, stole people's sandwiches, spurned their steaks, chased their dogs and cats—and they loved it. Jan was horrified. "And they think he is *cute?*" she'd say, dumbfounded.

It was Tabasco's perky brashness that most people found unbelievable. At Sasamat Lake he met a HORSE. We were quietly poking our way along the beach with Tabasco skipping in and out of the holes he was digging when the horse walked up and stood right over him. The horse and its rider towered over Tabasco like a mountain but the raccoon wasn't fazed a bit. He danced over to the horse's legs, pawed its hooves, then bounced away to dig in a hole. Back he went again to the horse and, this time, stretched up as far as he could towards the horse's knees. I was scared, the rider was scared, but not Tabasco. As the raccoon stretched up, the horse stretched down to meet him and they rubbed noses. Even my sister was proud of the raccoon that day.

Yet he was unpredictable. Sometimes, like later that afternoon, he reverted to his babyhood ways. It seemed that he could take on the world only when he knew I was near.

Jan and I chose a sunny little knoll at the end of the lake for our picnic, and while she guarded the food from attack I went for a swim.

"Don't leave me here too long with this monster," she pleaded.

"No worries, mate. Tabasco isn't taking any notice of us, he's exploring the salal bushes and picking berries."

Well, he *was*. But by the time I had swum a hundred yards from shore he was running up and down the beach, scrambling over rocks and paddling through reeds. I was getting too far away from him and he didn't like it. To add to his troubles, a flock of cheeky crows followed him along the shoreline, croaking and dive-bombing. He churred in alarm, more worried about the distance that separated us than about being bugged by crows.

As I left the log I was floating on to swim to shore, Tabasco dived into the water. Semi-submerged and with only his pointed head showing above the water, he looked like a little submarine. He was heading directly towards me. I was torn between giving him comfort and keeping afloat. It wasn't so bad if he rode on my back but he wasn't crazy, he always climbed on my head, the highest point and the furthest out of the water. The water was deep, and at ten pounds Tabasco could drown me.

I veered off to the right but he swerved with me. I veered to the left and he did the same thing. Then, with the crows still cawing above him at the unusual sight, he caught up to me and clung tightly to my bathing cap. I tried to shake him loose but he spread his body around my head and shoved his tail in my eyes till I feared I would lose my direction. Perhaps I was swimming to the centre of the lake instead of back to Jan. I gulped for air, swallowed water and, with the need for my own survival uppermost, I wrenched him off and beat it to shore. He was perfectly capable of swimming alone. He just needed the comfort of knowing his caretaker was near.

"Mom told me you were crazy," Jan said once again

as the raccoon and I dripped onto the beach. "She said I should look after you but you're as loony as the coon."

At last it was time to leave on our camping trip. I was looking forward to it but Jan was apprehensive.

"We're off tomorrow to the Rockies in the car with—you guessed it—Tabasco," she wrote to our parents. "And I'm worried. Lynette lets him roam all around the car when she's driving. She says after one patrol around the inside of the car he lies quietly on her lap or on the seat beside her. She reckons that he only becomes a nuisance if the passengers make a fuss and she stops him.

"Well, when I've been along, he is all over the car, on your head, under your feet, between the pedals, attacking you from behind. To get groceries home from the store Lynette has to put the bags in a cage. Otherwise, all you see is Tabasco's tail sticking up from the bottom of the bag. The rest of him is demolishing eggs, broccoli, chocolates, you name it. Can you imagine, bringing your stuff home from the store in a cage! I wonder how I'll be brought home from the Rockies.

"Pray for me.

"Your loving daughter, Jan."

Sometimes, I did have trouble with Tabasco in the car. His fingers would find the tiniest tear in things like the plastic door lining, the upholstery or the steering wheel cover, and he wasn't content till he'd made the tear bigger. If he saw something sticking out, like electrical wiring, he'd not rest till he'd pulled it to its limit. If I left him in the car while I was shopping or visiting, he'd honk the horn till somebody came along to keep him company.

But Tabasco loved some things about car travel. He loved the wind. If he couldn't squeeze out the window he'd lean out and try to catch the wind in his hands. He'd close his eyes and feel it flatten his whiskers and curl his lip into a leer. He liked the draft that blew through the air vents, too. He'd go to sleep lying on his back beside the vent with all four paws standing straight up in the air.

I hated putting Tabasco in a cage but I realized I couldn't let him loose around the car while travelling with Jan through two provinces. As expected, he screamed like a rooster for the first couple of days and vented his indignation on the upholstery, any of it that he could reach through the bars.

"He's a spoiled brat, you know," said Jan, watching me turn around in the seat and drop cookies in front of him to distract his attention from what was left of the car's plastic lining. "You'll want me to cuddle him next."

"Actually, I do. He's not used to being penned up and he's demanding a lot more attention now you're here with me. Animals get jealous just like people do."

Tabasco liked some people and disliked others, and he sensed when they liked or disliked him. He really liked men with beards or moustaches, especially if they had long hair. He loved running his fingers through their hair and separating the strands. He liked children. Sometimes, he'd choose one he specially liked and invite that person for a game. He'd jump up and down, twirl in the air and, with mouth wide open, make little "huh, huh, huh" sounds as if to say, "Come on, let's have fun." He didn't like children who screamed or teased. He'd growl and leap at them, which of course made them scream even more.

With three of us living so close together on this trip, Jan and Tabasco had to get along even if they didn't get to like each other. We worked out some arrangements that helped. I kept Tabasco in the cage while we were travelling in the car and in a cat harness while we went sightseeing in towns or stopped at roadside beauty spots. He hated the leash as much as the cage and such was his ability to manipulate himself out of it with his dexterous little fingers that he wore it around his stomach instead of his chest. He looked pretty funny waddling through a shopping mall but it was handy when Jan insisted we go into a store by ourselves. I could commandeer mall visitors into hanging on to a leash more easily than wrestling an animal into their arms. A box of playthings usually kept Tabasco near their feet.

Sometimes storekeepers put sweets on their counters to entice Tabasco into their stores then asked us to put on our show. I laughed and explained that we weren't a circus or a travelling roadshow. We were just on our summer vacation.

I let Tabasco off the leash if we stayed at a campground because he stopped bugging Jan and went around visiting other campers. They all thought he was wild or somehow belonged to the campsite. Tabasco loved hamming it up to a campground audience and they loved him. With him wandering the campsite, Jan and I were free to set up the tent, get a meal ready and prepare the sleeping bags without a raccoon getting in the way.

We all slept together. Fortunately, Tabasco was used to sleeping on my pillow at home or snuggling down under the sheets in my bed so he was content to do that on the ground in my sleeping bag. Jan didn't have to worry about him snooping into her bag. Still, she zipped up the bag as far as she could and buried her head in it, just in case.

"Everybody but me seems to like Tabasco," Jan confessed to Mom and Dad in her next letter. "He makes friends wherever we go, whether it's a shop girl in the Okanagan or a camper in the Rockies. I guess he knows how I feel. I had to hold him when a TV interviewer stopped us along the road to ask us how we liked our vacation. I must have been distracted by the scenery because for one second I went off coon alert and that awful raccoon got my thumb and I could have sworn I had lost it.

"Then next morning I was sitting in my nightie having breakfast by a lovely stream thinking this wilderness wasn't so bad after all when Tabasco landed on my head from the bough above. I lost my breakfast: lovely peaches we'd picked ourselves from an orchard in the Okanagan, muesli (they call it granola here), eggs, toast—he swiped the lot. Lynette started laughing. By the mischievous look on his face I think Tabasco laughed too. They both thought it was a great joke."

Actually, food was something Tabasco and Jan had in common. They both loved sweet stuff, not only Apple Jacks and Froot Loops, but sweet cookies, sticky donuts, cinnamon buns, chocolates and chocolate sundaes. "But they're not GOOD for you," I wailed, trying to interest them in chicken instead.

"There are grizzly bears in this country," continued Jan in her letter. "Lynette says that they don't come near camps unless there's food around. But we do have food around. Lynette keeps chicken and crayfish in the icebox in the car for the raccoon. I wonder, can bears smell chicken through a car door? And do you think they eat raccoons?"

One morning Jan saw animal tracks around our campsite and, when another camper confirmed they were bear tracks, she flatly refused to spend another night in a tent. She marched up to the reception desk at Château Lake Louise and booked a room. We'd already spent one night in a hotel where I'd kept Tabasco in the bathroom. When he screamed I let him out into the room but Jan insisted she could not sleep with him roaming freely. So I spent that night with the cage beside my bed and my hands through the bars to keep Tabasco company.

I intended to do the same in Château Lake Louise but Jan chose a room without a bathroom attached and I didn't see how I could smuggle the cage to the fourteenth floor. I remembered that pet raccoons weren't welcome in Alberta. Perhaps people wouldn't mind because this hotel was in a national park and animals were protected, but I didn't want to chance it if they did. There was only one thing to do and that was to leave Tabasco in the car in the car park.

"Before I leave the raccoon in the car all night we

have to take him for a walk, okay?" I said to my sister when we settled in.

"Not me. I'm going to stay right here and enjoy my beautiful room in peace. I'm going to put on my makeup, get into my best dress, have a proper dinner with a choice of delicious desserts and forget that raccoon. I don't mind wilderness if I can see it from a luxury hotel."

The next night we drove the Icefields Parkway to the Athabasca Glacier for Jan to see a glacier close at hand. After her experience at Château Lake Louise she was determined to stay at the Icefield Chalet. I'd given up hope of getting her out with Tabasco on a trek through the mountains with our packsacks, dried food and pup tent. It looked as if we'd have to stick to more beaten trails.

"We're fully booked, sorry," said the lady behind the reception desk of the Icefield Chalet. "But you can camp just over there."

I almost felt sorry for my sister as she prepared for another night out in the open in bear country. Trouble was, I couldn't help laughing. If a bear had stumbled into our tent he probably would have been bowled over by surprise at one camper dressed in a live raccoon fur and the other dressed in curlers, a face mask and fashionable lacy lingerie. Ours was not a typical wilderness tent scene.

Actually, our time at the Athabasca Glacier was one of the highlights of the trip—for both Jan and Tabasco.

"Excuse me, I'm looking for my raccoon. Have you seen him?" I asked the nice-looking man bending over the campfire.

"Are you kidding?" he said with a laugh.

"No, he's out exploring but it's time for supper." The man still didn't seem to believe me so I felt I had to introduce myself.

"You're not Lyn Hancock, the writer of books about animals, are you? We've read all of them."

When I nodded he called excitedly, "Hey, Fiona, Lyn Hancock's here and she's lost her raccoon."

Bill and Fiona Day were camping in a tent trailer with their two children, Simon and Penny, and their part terrier, part cocker spaniel, James.

"I hope you don't mind James," said Fiona chattily in a very English voice. "Being a dog he'll probably beat up on your raccoon so I'll pen him up till you find him."

"I hope you don't mind Tabasco," I laughed. "He's got a habit of snooping into everything." I didn't tell them that I thought it more likely that Tabasco would beat up on James if it came to a fight.

"We'd love to have you and your raccoon visit us tonight for coffee in the tent trailer," Fiona prattled on enthusiastically. "Simon and Penny will be thrilled to bits. And I'd love to get your autograph for my mother in England."

"Thank you. If you don't mind I'll bring my sister. She's visiting from Australia and is not used to this camping stuff, especially with a raccoon. I'd like her to know there are some more animal nuts in the world."

Just then, Tabasco chittered from a nearby pine tree. He never missed out on an invitation although usually he just barged in on his own.

With Bill, Jan, Tabasco and me on one side and Fiona, Penny, Simon and James knee to knee on the other side, it was a tight squeeze in the tent trailer. The Day family was terrified that James and Tabasco would get into a fight. James was throttling himself on a short lead trying to get close enough to investigate this stranger in his home while Tabasco, not one bit worried, scampered around the trailer as if he owned it.

Much to the delight of the Days, the raccoon went to each of them in turn and patted their faces with his soft paws. He opened their mouths, fingered their teeth and fished into their ears and noses. Much to the delight of Jan, he left her alone. He remembered the rules. Every time he landed near her, he skidded to a stop and you could hear him thinking, "Not her again."

"What's he eat?" asked Simon.

"A lot of things at home but he's not as interested in food now we're doing all this travelling. I like to give him whole foods like sardines or chicken but he prefers junk food."

"We've got a can of sardines here, let's try him on that," suggested Fiona.

"And we could put a sardine in the pouch of this windcheater I'm wearing. He's been probing around in it already," continued Bill.

Sardines on clothes may not have been the best idea in terms of bear safety, but it worked as far as Tabasco was concerned. Tabasco sat on Bill's shoulder and wiggled inside his pocket till his ferreting fingers latched onto the sardine. Everybody then wanted to put sardines in their pockets or up their sleeves or down their shirts to attract Tabasco's attention. He went from one to another, fishing out sardines, sucking them down head to tail SLUCK, SLUCK, SLUCK and leaving oily paw prints in his wake. Jan looked aghast. She tried to squeeze herself even tighter into a corner of the trailer. "Our clothes were a little revolting after that," Fiona confessed later.

The next morning it snowed.

Having lived in Canada for half my life, snow didn't excite me, though it was a surprise to see it in summer. But for Jan and Tabasco it was their first experience. While I struggled with bacon and eggs on the camp-fire, they both ran around, squealing in excitement and sticking their tongues out to catch the falling flakes. Jan forgot about cold and her ladylike ways and scampered about in the snow in negligee and curlers yelling, "Snow! Snow! Snow! I've never seen snow." Tabasco, more suit-ably dressed in fur, romped beside her, chittering and squeaking as the snow piled up.

"You all look as if you're having fun," Fiona laughed as she came to visit. "I've left my family to cook their own breakfast. I'm more fascinated with yours."

Later that day Jan went for a ride up the glacier in a Sno-Cat. I stayed to walk Tabasco through the snow so he could practise snowshoeing. He had brought his own snowshoes with him in the form of two pairs of flat feet. Not too many people rode the glacier with Jan on the Sno-Cat tour. They found that a naturally snowshoeing raccoon was far more fun.

The Days thought so too. "Come and visit us in

Vancouver as soon as you can," they called the next day as we said goodbye and headed home.

CHAPTER SIX

THERE'S A RACCOON IN MY APPLE ORCHARD

After Jan left Vancouver, Tabasco and I had to leave too. He was an illegal tenant in the apartment, he was getting older and he needed more room to explore. My first university project had finished but I was starting a new one in the Okanagan. Jack, my friend from the Fish and Wildlife Branch, had arranged for me to study cougars with him in the wild and to do a scientific study of a cougar in captivity. The landlady didn't want a raccoon. I was sure she wouldn't want a cougar.

Few raccoons live in the Okanagan area of British Columbia—it is on the edge of their range—so I didn't intend to release Tabasco there when he grew up. But by setting up an office at Jack's place in the middle of an orchard by Trout Creek in Summerland, the raccoon would be free to explore trees, fields, hills and a creek as soon as he stepped out the door. Okanagan Lake was just down the road. It was a good place for him to practise living in the wild.

Jack lived in an old farmhouse with wide verandas.

Most of the time Tabasco and I were there alone. Jack was away during the day with his work at Fish and Wildlife and then at night he was out trapping and tagging deer (orchardists were complaining that deer were eating their crops). Later, when snow was on the ground, he would be collaring cougars. Meanwhile, while waiting for cougar hunting season to begin and a baby cougar to be born at the local game farm, I would stay in my office in his farmhouse doing cougar research at a desk. And only Tabasco would be having fun.

Jack told me bluntly he didn't like raccoons. "They're nothing but trouble," he said. "They're destructive little beasts and cause problems. Tabasco should have been shot when his mother invaded human territory and went to live in that attic." He certainly didn't want Tabasco in his house—at least not while he was there—so he intended closing in the wide verandas as a kind of cage. I didn't want the raccoon in a cage but I realized there might be times when one was necessary. Actually, with the farmhouse ringed on two sides by wire, we would all be in a cage.

Before he got around to building the veranda cage, Jack built a separate cage at the back of the house by the creek. I put in an old stump and a lot of natural playthings like branches and rocks, and left the door open. Perhaps Tabasco would spend the winter in the hollow tree stump as the zoo raccoons did. I made a habit of putting his food and water dishes inside so he would associate at least something pleasant with being in a cage. Jack kept reminding me that Tabasco had five times more space than zoo raccoons did. True, but I didn't think Tabasco would see it that way.

Tabasco had the whole Okanagan if he wanted it. Perhaps because he was only five months old, he preferred staying close to home, especially when home was so new. Every day I would shoo him out of the house and settle down in my office and every day he would tear holes in the front screen door to try to get in. Jack wasn't too happy about mending it.

I tried leaving it open so the raccoon could see that even if he tore down the screen door, he still had a wooden door barring his way into my office. But raccoons are persistent, especially Tabasco, and he just swung back and forth on the screen door, chittering to come in. Often I wouldn't hear his cries above the noise of the electric typewriter and he would give up and sleep on the step, wedged between the two doors.

But he would wake immediately and bound to the other side of the house if I opened the back door. Before I could close it again, he'd dive under my feet and rush into the kitchen. He knew exactly where he was going —behind the fridge.

"Huhuh! You're bigger now, you can't fit," I said gleefully, making a grab for his bushy tail.

But Tabasco eluded my grasp and rushed into the living room to squeeze under the chesterfield. I lay down, cheek against the carpet, but he always moved out of reach of my groping fingers.

"Okay, you little monster, why don't you explore the house and get that out of your system. If I can't beat you,

you may as well join me. I'll teach you what you can touch and what you can't."

Life settled into a routine. Each morning I shooed him into the orchard and hoped he would climb a tree or go paddling in the creek. Then, when this didn't work, I let him into the office. After an initial outburst of discovery, he settled down happily with the garbage box. In fact, I gave him several garbage boxes and he was content to spend hours beside my desk turfing out empty packets, crumpling up paper balls, pulling refills out of pens and chucking things everywhere. He'd bury himself in clouds of paper then throw them up in the air like autumn leaves. When Tabasco got bored with that, he'd hoist himself on my lap, wriggle into his favourite position and go to sleep.

I didn't mind this routine as there was nothing breakable in the garbage boxes and it took only minutes to scoop up their contents and put them back before Jack came home.

You have to accept priorities when raising a raccoon. You have to balance the pleasure and the pain. You learn to put up with toilet rolls in the toilet bowl and torn weather stripping on the car door letting in the rain. In exchange you get the warm little snort of recognition and purring welcome when the raccoon greets you after an absence or its trusting vulnerability as it lies on its back with all four legs in the air and goes to sleep.

Some wild creatures, such as coyotes, foxes, opossums, squirrels and, yes, especially raccoons, become accustomed to living near people and they raise their young in the same way of life. Tabasco's mother was an urban raccoon and perhaps she passed on the tendency to want to be with people to her son.

When the apple pickers arrived at our side of the orchard, Tabasco turned his attention to them. I thought this was a marvellous opportunity to work by myself in a neat tidy office but it didn't work out that way.

Tabasco loved climbing up and down ladders. Sometimes, he'd climb up behind the apple pickers and sit on their shoulders and swing their buckets while they were picking. Other times he'd squeeze past them, crawl out to the end of a branch, clutch the thin end with all four paws in his usual upside down position and knock off apples himself. Few people deny a raccoon's intelligence —even Jack—so perhaps Tabasco was trying to help.

The apple pickers didn't appreciate it. I could hear what they thought of such help in their screams—right over the noise of the typewriter. I rushed outside and tried to help them myself by catching the apples before they fell to the ground. I thought Tabasco and I made a good team with him picking them and me catching them.

The men didn't think so. Tabasco didn't always pick them clean. Occasionally, he bit into them and left his investigative teeth marks. I thought a label on such apples like "These apples were picked by a raccoon" would add to their value but the men didn't think that was a good idea either.

"My pickers are worried they'll fall off their ladders with a raccoon climbing around their necks filching apples from their baskets," said their supervisor. "And they don't get paid for apples that get bruised when they hit the ground."

It wasn't the apples that Tabasco was interested in so much as the people picking them. Except for denting a few tomatoes and slapping some beets around, he largely ignored Jack's vegetable garden because Jack was rarely in it to keep him company.

So Tabasco had to come inside with me or be locked up in the cage outside until picking season was over. Raccoons are well known for their ability to get out of things, whether rooms or boxes, cars or cages. Tabasco was a magician in the various ways he outsmarted Jack's strategies to keep him inside that cage. He could lift up the wire, gnaw through wood, tunnel under dirt and pick locks. "He can turn in his skin, the little devil," Jack said with grudging admiration.

Just as the raccoon was adept at getting out of the cage, so was he clever at getting inside the house. Jack had to board up the doors and windows. He grumbled but he had to admit that Tabasco had brains, excellent powers of observation, tremendous strength and agility and remarkable perseverance. He was developing respect for raccoons. He even said that Tabasco was interesting to have around the house—not in the house, he emphasized, but around the house.

As fall wore on, the fruit and the leaves disappeared from the trees, leaving big holes in the landscape so that Tabasco could see people on the road or walking through the orchard—and people could see him.

One day, Todd, one of the neighbour boys who had

heard about the raccoon, came over and introduced himself. He was a little blond boy of about nine who was used to animals. Great, I thought, he can be the first of my raccoon-sitters in the Okanagan. Todd diked the irrigation flume to make a waterfall and Tabasco went head over forepaws in excitement as he sloshed and splashed around in the water and leapt up to catch the spray. With Todd running beside him, he skipped along the flume, jumped down, climbed up again on the wooden trestle, and skipped through the water some more. He stood up in the water as it was rushing under him and tugged at the waxberries that grew alongside. This was a fun kind of bathtub.

Tabasco liked Todd so much that he tried to follow him home. He chased the boy through the orchard and down the trail to the road. Compared to Hastings Street, the road that ran by the orchard was quiet and isolated but I didn't want Tabasco exploring it till we did it together. The raccoon would have to learn some traffic sense first. I called him back and Todd got on his bike to outstrip Tabasco and discourage him from following him farther.

On most days Tabasco and I would go for a walk. The raccoon would scamper merrily through the long grass under the orchard trees and bowl over peaches and bite into apples, but when we reached the road, he'd stick close to my feet. The road was unfamiliar territory and there were new dogs and cats to handle and new people to meet.

Beauregard, Jack's friendly old springer spaniel, would

come with us. Poor Beauregard was always striving to get people's attention and was always being ignored. He lifted people's hands with his head for a do-it-yourself pat. He threw sticks. He rubbed against people's legs, he looked at them with soulful, doleful eyes, he slobbered over them with licks and kisses—but people always made more of a fuss over Tabasco.

The raccoon teased him unmercifully. He jumped on top of him, pulled his tail, tugged at his ears, stole his dog food and tipped over his water dish. Beauregard never seemed to mind. He remained loyal and loving.

Up till now, Tabasco had been able to bully the city dogs, but some of the country dogs were more difficult to handle. The raccoon treated them in the same way: he fingered their faces, parted their hair, chewed their ears and bit their legs. But country dogs tended to bite back.

Tabasco puffed himself into his hedgehog position to send a yappy little white poodle flying home, but even a growl and a tail lashing did nothing to stop the big black police dog from nosing him into a corner. The raccoon greeted me with a funny little whine that I took as thanks when I came up to rescue him.

One day, two dogs—a German shepherd and a black Lab—ganged up on Tabasco as he was galloping cockily through the orchard ahead of me. They jumped on top of him and, by sheer weight and size, buried him in the grass. Growling was no use to him now and he could scarcely put his back up when he was hidden somewhere under his attackers. In fact, his back was on the ground. Suddenly, Beauregard, barking loudly, shot out from behind me and made a dive for the dogs. Thinking I would lose both the spaniel and the raccoon, I rushed forward myself but Beauregard had things in hand. While Beau drove off the dogs, Tabasco saw his opportunity and climbed the nearest tree. It was the first time I caught the smell of fear from his scent glands.

From then on, Tabasco treated other dogs with a little more caution. He still went up to tap them on the face but he was ready to leave the moment they showed they didn't want to be bugged. And Beauregard, enjoying his new role as benefactor to the raccoon, got more than one dog by the throat when he thought it would threaten his friend. Tabasco didn't seem to give him any thanks.

When we reached the road at the end of our orchard we had two choices: uphill to Giant's Head and Anne's orchard or downhill to Okanagan Lake. Uphill was a big puff for Tabasco and Anne wasn't too happy with a raccoon that interrupted her plum picking and pruning. The men were a little apprehensive of Tabasco's habit of climbing up the ladder, clawing past their jeans to get to the top rung then going to sleep in their buckets of plums. If any of the orchardists' pet dogs or cats came to investigate, Tabasco would puff himself into his fighting position and everybody got nervous.

So we were more likely to go to the lake.

Cars rarely stopped along busy Vancouver streets, but here in Summerland, friendly country folk often stopped when they saw Tabasco romping along the side of the road.

"Hey, can I take a picture?" one man shouted, leaning out the truck window and flourishing a camera as he passed.

"Excuse me, please, but I'd love to show my mother your raccoon," said a lady, stopping the car beside us.

Tabasco needed no second invitation to clamber into a car. He felt right at home, especially in one with no cage. He climbed over the seats and over the passengers, ate candy and spread the sticky wrappers in their hair, very funny to everybody except the person who owned the hair. And he always rifled purses. He was what he seemed—a regular highway bandit.

Another time, a well-dressed lady in pink, with a poodle in matching pink ribbons, stopped to chat.

"Ooh! What a dear little raccoon! May I introduce it to my Timmy?" she gushed.

Tabasco did a quick size-up of Timmy, decided he could handle him as he had the city dogs and jumped inside her car. Timmy didn't look so sure. Any raccoon he had seen before had been in a zoo. Those strange masked creatures seemed safer behind bars. The poodle retreated to his mistress's lap. Tabasco, attracted to the shiny pendant hanging from her neck, followed the poodle to feel the pendant but I intervened before there was any more excitement.

Obviously, word of a raccoon living in the orchard at Trout Creek had got around. "That's the one," cried the man on the tractor trundling by. "The raccoon! The raccoon!" called the little girl on the seat behind him.

The noise of the tractor, an unfamiliar sound, sent Tabasco up the nearest tree. He made his way along a branch as usual but this one broke under his weight and he went crashing to the ground. Unhurt, he bounced up and grabbed an apple.

"Look at him, Daddy, he's trying to get his mouth around it, but it's too big," the little girl cried, pointing to Tabasco, who did look comical taking on an apple bigger than he could chew. He bounced on to another one and bit into that.

"I'm sorry," I said hastily to the man on the tractor. "I'll pay you for the apples."

"That's all right, they're already on the ground," he replied then laughed. "Anyway, they're not my apples."

If we turned right at the end of the road we reached the highway, a couple of shops, a school and the lake. By October, summer visitors to the Okanagan have gone home, children are in school and beaches are deserted. Tabasco, Beauregard and I usually had the lake to ourselves.

The raccoon loved it, especially on windy days when the golden leaves of the aspen trees blew onto the beach. He'd chase them into the water and swim out after them. Surprisingly, he took no notice of the ducks and geese that stopped to rest and feed on the lake before flying south. Unfortunately, Beauregard did. It seemed funny, a dog chasing ducks and a raccoon chasing leaves. Tabasco also chased waves. Smiling, with his mouth open making little "huhuhuh" squeaks, he'd skitter along the shore, pirouette like a ballet dancer, chase the waves, catch the spray then jump back in alarm as the waves splashed him on the nose. Unperturbed, he'd always go back for more.

He loved playing in the sand too. He dug holes, burrowed down inside, then turned around at the bottom and came up covered with sand from whiskers to tail.

In strange territory Tabasco always followed me, but in country he knew, Beauregard and I followed Tabasco. One of his favourite stopping places on the way home was the school. He liked climbing the fence and, like a gymnast doing beam exercises, he practised walking along the top railing. His naturally rolling gait helped him balance. If kids were out in the playground having their lunch, he'd refuse handouts and steal from their lunch pails instead.

Chasing beetles, crickets and grasshoppers kept Tabasco busy in the long grass under the fruit trees. And sometimes, when we came back by the creek, he'd pounce on frogs. As fall progresses, raccoons instinctively eat more to prepare themselves for winter and Tabasco doubled his weight in his first month in the Okanagan.

On Halloween, Tabasco and I went trick-or-treating with Anne's son, Lorne. The raccoon had no need to disguise himself, he wore his own mask naturally, but Lorne came dressed as the Frankenstein monster. When we went to pick him up, Tabasco saw Lorne in his flowing black robes and gargoyle-toothed mask come running towards the car and immediately fled under my seat. For a long time, not even candy would draw him out. He was also scared of big fat jack-o'-lanterns with candles inside them. This was surprising because in a house he was always looking for boxes of matches, pouches of tobacco, packets of cigarettes and pipe cleaners.

Lorne had collected quite a bag of goodies before Tabasco emerged from his hiding place and ventured out to go trick-or-treating. Both the boy and the raccoon went up to a door together. And then, surprisingly, it wasn't the candies or apples the raccoon was interested in but the house itself. As soon as the door was opened, he scuttled inside and instinctively made for the bathroom, dragged the toilet roll to the toilet, dunked it in and turned on the taps. People would be left standing on their doorsteps with bags and mouths open while Frankenstein chased a masked bandit inside. They had no chance to choose a treat over a trick.

Tabasco seemed to like living in Trout Creek. He got lots of attention. Todd or some of the other neighbour kids came after school each day to play with him or take him for a walk along the irrigation flume. With winter approaching, the flume water had been cut off and orchardists got their water from underground pipes. But the aqueduct led up the creek a few miles to a dam in a gully between sandy sidehills, and here there were more interesting places for a raccoon to explore.

Sometimes, Tabasco and Beauregard went exploring by themselves. With more companions, the raccoon spent less time swinging on the screen door and this made Jack happy.

"He's an interesting character, I must admit," Jack said one day, "but I am trying hard not to like him because he has to be ready to live in the wild."

"Raccoons adapt to living in cities with people so well," I'd sometimes argue, "that I don't see why I can't have Tabasco live with me the way Beauregard lives with you. Why is it considered bad to have a wild pet and okay to have a domesticated pet? A wild pet is far more independent and interesting. And it's not as if Tabasco is kept in a cage."

"You're going to have problems," Jack said darkly. "Just wait and see."

We had a minor problem the following Sunday. Because he was away a lot, Jack treated his Sunday dinner at home as sacred. He cooked it and he demanded that his guests were prompt to the table and ate it while it was hot. Just as Jack was putting the roast turkey on the table, Anne phoned.

"Lyn, the raccoon is down at the gas station on the highway. He followed some kids home. The gas station owner tried to shoo him in your direction but he was having too much fun getting in and out of people's cars when they drove up for gas. You'd better go get him."

"Well, that's Sunday dinner ruined," Jack grumbled as I got in the car.

I didn't have to go as far as the gas station. Tabasco had taken a lift halfway home and when we picked him up, he was humping down the trail like a little Cadborosaurus or the Loch Ness monster. He looked as if he knew he was late and he was hurrying to get home for Sunday dinner himself.

Usually, Tabasco came when he was called. About suppertime I would stand out on the veranda and yell, "Tabasco-o-o" and then wait. Minutes might pass but usually he would appear at my heels like a little black ghost.

Sometimes, however, other people would bring him home. They all thought he must have got out of his cage. Most of them were thrilled to be visited by a raccoon.

The man who lived in the house at the end of the trail brought Tabasco home in his car. "Your coon was into my carrots," he said offhandedly, as if it didn't matter to him at all.

The furnace-oil man said, "I always wanted a raccoon for a pet. He's a thief, though, always into my pockets. What's he looking for?"

Todd's mother told me Tabasco liked riding around on her husband's head and bouncing up and down on her waterbed. "Do you think his claws might go through, though?" she asked a little worriedly.

One night a farmer phoned. "I think I have something you may be looking for. A couple of boys dropped off a raccoon here a few hours ago. They thought this was where it lived. It dived into a bucket of barnacles and mussels my son just brought from the coast. If it's yours, what is it supposed to eat?"

"Chicken," I said, unthinkingly.

"Oh, er..." He choked a bit then said cautiously, "I have a chicken farm."

"Don't worry, he eats chicken from the supermarket. He runs away from live chickens. I'll be down to pick him up."

It was true. He showed no interest in chasing birds—perhaps that was because he had been brought up beside pigeons, starlings and gulls. I fed him grapes, nuts, dog food and chicken, and he scrounged for himself as well, in the country eating berries, windblown apples and peaches, grasshoppers and frog larvae, and in the city eating crabs, fish and crayfish. But contrary to what wild raccoons are supposed to do, Tabasco took the longest time to learn how to eat an egg. He rolled it, chased it, batted it. He picked it up and held it in his hands. He tried to roll it around between his palms. He tried to bite it, the method wild raccoons use to get into eggs. Tabasco's eggs remained intact.

Finally one day he pressed an egg against cement and it broke. Then, as if he had been doing it all his life, he slurped up the yolk and the white till the shell was dry.

CHAPTER SEVEN

THERE'S A RACCOON UNDER MY CHRISTMAS TREE

In the wild, raccoons of Tabasco's age would be looking for a cozy den to spend the winter. He already had one in a tree stump in his cage in the Okanagan, but he rarely spent time there of his own accord. He preferred visiting the neighbours.

He liked wandering the orchard and poking into the outbuildings to look for a high, secluded ledge to have a snooze. He had no intention of sleeping there all winter. Following the feet of children as they walked to and from school or playing on patios while their parents watched through the security of their glass doors was far more fun. He regularly visited half a dozen neighbours in a mile-wide circle.

Most of them didn't mind his visits and some of them, especially the closest ones like Todd's parents, were delighted when Tabasco made their sheds into his second homes. Todd continued to take the raccoon for walks along the creek. His father, Gary, carried Tabasco around on his shoulder while he did chores, and his mother, Carole, let him come to her coffee parties. The family was very concerned for the raccoon's welfare.

"Tabasco fell off the rafters of the woodshed today. That's higher than a ceiling," Gary said in wonderment. "I felt sure he'd get hurt. It knocked the wind out of him but he landed on the snow and picked right up again."

Other neighbours, thinking he was lost, phoned to let me know where he was. "No, he's not a nuisance but he wants in so badly. It seems so cold now for him out in the orchard." Those who fell for Tabasco's pleading eyes on the porch and let him inside confessed afterwards that "it was a mistake."

Tabasco wanted to be indoors for the sake of company, not because of the cold. He was in excellent health, over twenty pounds in weight, and he had a shiny warm fur coat. Like wild raccoons in the fall, he had developed a taste for nuts, which helped pad him with fat for the winter season. He had doubled his weight in the Okanagan.

Tabasco loved flying into the living room to the nut jar on the coffee table. At first, he leaned over the table, scooped out two handfuls of nuts from deep in the bowl and, without looking what he was doing, scooted under the chesterfield to devour them in peace. Later, he got brave enough to jump right onto the table. Once when he thought I was going to stop him, he curled his fingers individually around half a dozen nuts of various sizes and stuffed them into his mouth. All were gone in a flash.

At first, he bit into each nut one piece at a time and made a terrible mess sending shells and nutmeats every which way. Then he learned to bite them in two with just the right pressure to break the shell cleanly and reveal the whole nut inside. Eventually, he learned how to break an egg the same way, not by pressing it against something hard but by biting into the shell.

There were lots of Tabasco's favourite goodies around at Christmastime. He did his rounds collecting nuts, chocolates, eggs and mandarin oranges. He'd go off during the day on his social calls then at dark I'd stand on the veranda and call him. He made no answering call but suddenly, as if from nowhere, he'd appear at my feet, silent and ghostlike. It was eerie.

On Christmas Eve I stopped work at the typewriter for a two-day holiday. This evening, usually, Tabasco didn't come to my call. I pulled on my parka and mukluks and went to look for him. I knew he had to be with people. Trouble was, Christmas Eve was not a good night of the year for a people-loving raccoon to be wandering from party to party.

Gary, Carole and Todd were away and the people looking after their house for the holiday hadn't seen Tabasco. There was a lot of light and noise and laughter from a house on the creek way down at the end of the orchard, but, as I hadn't been to it before or even seen it in summer through the trees, I searched instead in the opposite direction. Tabasco usually wandered down the trail to the road.

"Yes, Tabasco was here earlier," said the couple in the first house. "We were taking pictures of him." The raccoon had left the evidence. Smudge marks on the patio door. Plastic torn off the windows. Stuffing ripped from the upended kitchen chairs.

The elderly man in the house next door had chickens and, knowing Tabasco's love for eggs, I didn't really want to check there. But he was very welcoming. "No, he didn't come here tonight, but I'm glad you did, I wanted to meet you. I do hope he doesn't get hurt. There's a lot of crazy drivers out tonight," he said. "Oh, do you want to take some eggs home for Tabasco? They can be his Christmas present from me."

Bertha, who lived in the third house, was away but her dogs, two big Dalmatians, barked madly as I passed. Tabasco had learned to fear dogs in the Okanagan and, with Beau not at his side to protect him, I was sure he'd sidestepped their place.

The fourth house was dark and empty. No fun there. I continued on as I knew Tabasco would.

The people who were looking after the Palmberg house were having a very lively party but the family Tabasco knew were away. In fact, most of the regular people on his circuit were either gone or had other people staying in their houses.

By the time I had checked a few more houses along Tabasco's usual route and reached the highway, I was beginning to be concerned—and not only for Tabasco. Jack was waiting for his Christmas Eve dinner and I had planned to cook it. I had been tramping through the snow in the dark for almost two hours.

"I expected it," Jack said resignedly when I phoned. "I stayed in old clothes in case you wanted me to join you in the search."

Wondering whether or not I should phone the local radio and police stations, I trudged back to Jack's place. Moonlight was now shining over the creek and onto our veranda. I looked down at the glistening snow and saw stuffing. Not the stuffing to be put in the Christmas turkey but the kind of stuffing raccoons shred from kitchen chairs.

I was on the right trail, a stuffing trail, and it led through the trees along the creek to the noisy house at the end of the orchard. I stumbled across a garden of snow-crusted winter cabbages and threaded through sheds, garages and other outbuildings to a cozy cedar house with wide patio doors.

This was where the action was on Christmas Eve in Trout Creek. And judging by the laughter, shouting, applause and delighted screams, Tabasco had found it.

"Toon, toon, tatoon," I heard some toddler cry as I rang the bell.

"So you own the raccoon," said the nice lady who answered the door. "Come in, I'm Katy Madsen. We're having a ball with this raccoon."

I knew Katy by reputation. She was a local naturalist and a well-known animal lover. Sensibly, she had not invited Tabasco into the house and he was doing his entertaining on a table in the glassed-in porch. His audience was entranced. They blew whistles, waved their party hats and clapped while he danced and pranced and whirled and twirled on the other side of the glass. Tabasco was the life of the party and he loved it. No wonder he hadn't wanted to come home when I called.

But supper was waiting and there were presents to be opened. I hoisted the hero on my shoulder and he rode off to a final round of applause, clinging to my parka hood with one hand and eating Katy's chocolates with the other. He was still smiling and making his little "uhuh, uhuh" noises when we got back home.

Next day, we had a Christmas dinner party and gift opening for the animals down at the creek. Our guests were Shelley, Jack's twelve-year-old daughter who was visiting us for the Christmas holidays, Tabasco and Beauregard.

I hung gaily wrapped boxes of dog food meaties, mandarin oranges, nuts, juicy bones and boxes of Apple Jacks on the bare branches overhanging the creek and Tabasco either stretched up on the ice and pulled them down or else he walked along the limbs and pulled them up. Then he had the fun of tearing into the packages, shredding the paper, and ripping out the contents. This was the raccoon's first Christmas and he must have wondered why he was allowed to do things that were definite no-no's in the office.

After dinner we played hockey on the partly frozen creek. Tabasco didn't need skates or sticks or pucks. He slipped and skidded over the ice, batting ice balls with his flat hands and feet. He splayed out his toes to get a better grip and waved his tail from side to side for better balance.

He used the same equipment when we went cross-country skiing with Shelley on weekends. At first, he wanted to stay in the car and bite Beauregard's ear but when we put on our skis and left him, he decided to follow. He plunged into the powder snow and floundered around till he found our tracks.

"He looks like a powder puff," said Shelley with a giggle as we turned around to watch Tabasco, spattered with snowflakes, humping after us with his shoulders hunched, tail waving and nose steadfastly pointed forwards. The tracks were deep—all we could see of him was his tail.

He made faster progress when we reached the snowmobile tracks. He stopped snowplowing and started galloping on the harder surface.

"Look!" called Shelley. "He's heading away to that tree. He's making his own tracks."

The courageous little raccoon was in strange country but he recognized a tree, the only one in this vast expanse of whiteness, and he wanted to climb it. He left the main trail and pushed through virgin snow to a huge ponderosa pine hung with pale green lichen. We rested on our skis and watched while he tried to climb the smooth, icy bark. With all four limbs splayed outward as far as they could go, he snatched jerkily at the tree to propel himself upwards the way a logger does. Unfortunately, not being able to hug the trunk with his arms as he did phone poles or the spindly fruit trees in the orchard, he kept slipping downwards.

"He's found some woodpecker holes," Jack told us, looking through his binoculars. "He's poking his fingers into them to haul himself up that way. Hmmm! Clever little coon."

Raccoons have good memories. The ponderosa was a dead tree and Tabasco remembered from past experience that dead limbs could break under his weight. He made no attempt to walk along the side branches. Instead, he sat in a fork of the tree and chewed green lichen.

Jack could appreciate some raccoon abilities but he couldn't wait till Tabasco had tired of his tree. We had to push on. As the distance increased between us—and with Beauregard barking encouragement—the raccoon turned himself around on the trunk and descended. To slow his descent, he turned his hind feet backwards the way a squirrel does.

But curious raccoons are always being distracted. He suddenly veered off his freshly raccoon-plowed track and floundered through virgin snow again to a low gully.

"Well, I guess we have to ski where the raccoon goes," said Jack, a bit grimly.

When we got to where we last saw him, Tabasco was skating down the icy sides of the gully. He expected us to play with him. While Jack watched, Shelley and I kneaded snowballs into ice balls and rolled them down the bank like miniature avalanches. Tabasco slithered along the thin trail they made and tried to catch them.

"He can catch them okay," laughed Shelley. "Trouble is, he won't throw them back so we have to make some more."

Needless to say, after a day of snowshoeing, skiing and skating, Tabasco always slept in the car on the way home.

Jack didn't mind taking Tabasco with us when we

went skiing but he certainly refused to take the raccoon with us when we went collaring deer or cougars. One night he had no choice.

We were dining with friends and had taken Tabasco along. The Batkin family was high on his list of fans in the Okanagan. Art and Marg and their two children, Raymond and Donna, loved to babysit the raccoon in their trailer in Summerland.

While we were having dinner, Tabasco hung around on the steps outside. After dessert, the children begged to bring him in. Jack gave me a warning look but Art and Marg were as keen as their children to play with the raccoon.

"Just make sure you keep an eye on him," I advised, "and I mean all the time."

Tabasco needed no second invitation. As soon as the door opened, he scampered up the steps and, uncannily, headed for the bathroom. He ran right into a wooden wall. Standard procedure in partially raccoon-proofing a house while visiting is to close all doors to lessen the mess a raccoon can make. He pushed a case against the door and stood on it to reach the doorknob. He wiggled and shook and pulled it but it was smooth and his velvety hands kept slipping off the surface. Tabasco's last resort was to squeeze his fingers into the crack to pry the door open, but both the doorknob and the door refused to budge.

Well, if you can't get in one place, try another. The oven door had a handle. He cantered over to the stove, reached up to the oven door handle and pulled it downwards. Of course, it opened and came down on his nose so he gave that up. Ah, a cupboard above the stove. Tabasco knew a cupboard when he saw one and those doors opened sideways. "No, let him go, it's all right," Marg laughed when I leapt to head off a catastrophe. "Let's see what he likes."

Jack, who is usually concerned with more serious experiments, retreated to the corner with a newspaper. He threw up his hands as if he had seen it all before, which of course he had.

As expected, Tabasco made straight for the box of sugar cubes, filched a few in his mouth and slithered down the slippery kitchen counter to the floor. He lay on his back, all four feet in the air, and delicately rolled a single sugar cube around with all twenty toes. He did the same thing with ice cubes and grapes. Raccoons have marvellous control of small things, even things like ice and sugar cubes that get tinier and tinier the more they are handled.

After the explorations were done, Tabasco turned his constantly roving attention to the people. Art and Raymond immediately got down on the floor at raccoon level and let Tabasco climb all over their heads and pull their hair and finger their ears and noses. Donna, more cautious, donned her raccoon-attack gear of parka, mitts and toque before she joined them.

The play was interrupted by the telephone. The call was for Jack. There was a deer in his deer trap and we had to go and put a radio collar on it. There was no time to go home first so Tabasco had to come too.

"Just keep that raccoon out of the way," Jack warned

grimly as we headed for Trap Number Three on the hillside overlooking Peachland orchards.

Jack's truck was stuffed with trapping equipment, clothes, tools, canvas bags, radio collars and other gear for trapping and collaring deer. I couldn't let Tabasco loose in the truck. And I couldn't let him loose on the hill as he would be sure to interfere with the deer.

I found myself, raccoon in hand, shining a spotlight on a wildly thrashing doe with madly staring eyes while Jack worked to get it collared. I was sent scurrying back and forth between the trap and the truck to ferry his supplies.

"Get that goldarned raccoon away from me," yelled Jack as he struggled to keep the deer on the ground, avoid its violently flailing legs and circle its neck with the radio collar. "Find me short rivets, they're somewhere in the truck."

Alternately holding on to Tabasco's tail to keep him inside the truck and stuffing his head behind the seat to keep him away from the equipment, I scrabbled through jackets, boots, gloves, clipboards, plastic bags, Jack's pipe and tobacco and the rest of the jumble looking for short rivets. "I wish you knew what a rivet was, Tabasco, you'd find it like a shot," I said to the raccoon.

I think Tabasco thought this mess was made for him in some Raccoon Heaven or The Great Wastepaper Basket in the Sky. While Jack rode the deer around the trap, I rode Tabasco around the inside of the truck, lunging over the junk to keep hold of him. At one point, he broke away from my grasp and started crunching something under the seat. Rivets? Matches? Tranquilizers? No—cactus that had stuck to a pair of our boots. Tabasco was crunching cactus between his teeth with the same enthusiasm he showed for crunching Apple Jacks.

Finally, I found a bag of rivets but they were long.

"That's okay, I found the short ones in my pocket," said Jack as he finished fitting the collar around the doe's neck. "Now keep that raccoon clear while I let this doe go. She'll run uphill."

Still holding Tabasco, I took a position on the downside of the hill with my back to the road, the traffic, the orchards and the lake. I wanted to get a clear view of the deer as it escaped uphill in the moonlight.

But animals, like people, are unpredictable. "Watch out, Lyn, it's going downhill," yelled Jack.

Tabasco and I were nearly bowled over by the doe as it careered madly down the cactus-splashed slope, tore through a hole in the fence and leapt gracefully across the road to a lakeside orchard. From then on, its beeping radio collar would tell where it went.

Tabasco must have been miffed next day when we left him home and went off to radio collar a cougar in Shuttleworth Canyon. The back door had not been slammed tightly enough and we got back from our cougar hunt to find the farmhouse in chaos. The toilet bowl was plugged with toilet rolls, shampoo bottles, soap containers and toothpaste tubes. Blankets stripped from the beds and clothes pulled off hangers in the wardrobes filled the bathtub. The contents of kitchen cupboards were dragged upstairs and stuffed under the beds. A trail of Japanese noodles and broken necklaces linked the upstairs with the downstairs and made loops between the kitchen and the chesterfield in the living room.

"You know, I think Tabasco kept thinking someone was coming brandishing a big no-no stick so he kept hiding under the chesterfield. Then when he heard the truck drive up to the house, he raced outside rather than be caught inside. What do you think?" I asked Jack, innocently.

But Jack couldn't say anything. He was all choked up.

Tabasco continued his schooling and we continued ours. One day, he covered all grades from kindergarten to university.

Shelley, who was in grade six at Uplands Elementary in Penticton, took him to school and gave a little lecture on raccoons to each class as part of her wildlife appreciation project. I gave her a big lecture on how to stay out of trouble. She survived her day with Tabasco to tell me the highlights.

"In kindergarten the kids sat in a circle while Tabasco wandered around as if he owned the place. They were all smiles and giggles even when Tabasco crawled all over them. He nipped their ears, stole their nuts and threw their playthings out of the sandbox.

"I had to guard the teacher's desk in grade one because he opened her purse and upended her makeup bag.

"I put him in the sink in grade two so the kids could see how he turns taps on and catches the drips with his hands. Then I had to follow him around the room wiping up his wet paw prints.

"In grade three he tried nosing into the gerbil's cage and batting the gerbil but I didn't think I should put them together. He batted the cans and boxes around their play store instead.

"He batted a big ball around grade four.

"The grade fives were the best. They thought it was neat when Tabasco stood on the mice cage and it crushed under his weight. There were mice running everywhere and Tabasco was running everywhere trying to catch them. The class thought it was great."

"And the teacher?" I asked weakly.

"No sweat," replied Shelley cheerfully. "It took her some time but she caught all the mice. Tabasco got into a lot of trouble in grade six though. He was getting pretty rambunctious by this time with all the attention. He swiped everybody's bubblegum and I had a hard time getting it all back. He chewed a felt pen and got pink all over his tongue so I put him in a cage till lunchtime. I know you don't like him eating junk food but he really likes hot dogs and chips."

That night Jack and I took him to our wildlife course in Kelowna and learned a few things ourselves. The professor pried and poked and prodded then pronounced Tabasco to be a she, not a he. I had never questioned Tabasco's sex although I knew with raccoons it was difficult to tell. The zoo had said he was a he. The biologists at the Fish and Wildlife Branch had said he was a he. Jack had said he was a he.

"I wonder if I should change Tabasco's name to Tabasca," I said to Jack on the way back to Summerland.

"Think you could also change some of its ways?" Jack replied sweetly.

CHAPTER EIGHT

THERE'S A RACCOON EVERYWHERE

It was now spring in the Okanagan and Tabasco was almost a year old. In the wild, raccoons in this season are wandering off to find mates and living places of their own. One of the cougar hunters had recently seen another raccoon track in the area. Perhaps Tabasco would find a wild mate after all. Perhaps here in the country she would not become a nuisance as so many adult raccoons are in the city. I decided to experiment and not call Tabasco in at night.

She certainly seemed full of spring fever—chasing patient Beau, chasing her tail, chasing me, chasing the workers in the orchard again. "The pruners threw sticks at her today," Carole told me. "I got mad at them. I don't know what's wrong with them. We don't have any trouble with Tabasco."

"Well, maybe they can persuade Tabasco to stay away from them. He—I mean she—has to learn that not all humans are approachable. She's got to recognize the signals people put out—whom she can trust and whom she can't, whom she needs to avoid and whom she doesn't. She has to learn to fear some people for her own protection."

I wanted to protect Tabasco. I had taken on the responsibility of raising her when she was a baby, a time when everybody thought she was cute and adorable. I couldn't give up on my responsibility now that she was growing up and there were problems because some people didn't think she was cute anymore.

I looked at my options. First, I could protect her totally by locking her up in a cage and making sure she stayed there. Neither Tabasco nor I wanted that. Besides, she was in much better shape than the scruffy-looking zoo raccoons we'd seen. It didn't seem fair to let her run wild in the first part of her life then lock her up for the rest of her life as if she were some criminal whose only crime was growing up.

Second, I could drive out as far as I could in what was left of the wilderness and throw her out of the car to fend for herself. Lots of people do that with unwanted dogs and cats. These animals either starve to death or seek food, shelter and companionship from strangers who may or may not want to be bothered. I felt people would not want to handle a near adult raccoon, even in the Okanagan.

Third, I could let Tabasco decide for herself.

I had raised her to be a strong, healthy raccoon. I had introduced her to a variety of people, animals and experiences. I had helped her to learn how to live in the country yet take advantage of scrounging an extra living in the city. I had given her practice in getting out of dangerous situations, whether it was being attacked by a neighbour's dog or a stranger's truck or a tree pruner's stick or shovel. She had to learn for herself where she was welcome and where she was not. I could provide her with experience, a safe home and a lot of love, but the rest of her life was hers. She would have to take a chance. And that's really not much different than how it is in the human world.

Tabasco was free to come and go as she pleased. And as the buds burst into blossom in the orchard and everyone felt the need to get out of their houses and work in their yards or wander into wilder areas with a renewed zest for living, so did the raccoon. She'd stay out till midnight. I worried like any mother but she always came home, soaking wet and covered in mud, and I knew she'd spent a good deal of time in the creek. She was doing what the wild raccoons do in spring and summer, getting most of her food near water.

She chittered on the back step till I opened the door and then waddled into the kitchen at half the speed she'd left it in the morning. She stood on my lap, licked my face a few times and tried to pry open my mouth. Then, as if relaxing after a tough day, she lay on my lap with her back legs sticking straight up in the air and her front paws hanging limp. She was warm, cuddly, sleepy and very, very cute. Even Jack thought so. "That raccoon is best when she's asleep."

Occasionally, Tabasco stayed out overnight but she still came back in the morning. After a busy night she spent most of the next day sleeping under canvas in one of Gary's outbuildings. But now that more and more people were around, Tabasco sometimes joined them. The raccoon loved a party and rarely resisted the temptation of going to one, whether she was invited or not.

"Your raccoon's at a party in the garden opposite. I think she's drinking beer," one of the neighbours informed me over the phone. The thought of Tabasco as an underage drinker struck me as funny—I giggled at the idea of checking up on a teenager raccoon. But the caller had the raccoon's best interests at heart so I thanked her and hurried towards the party. Todd caught up with me in the orchard and we went together.

People were obviously enjoying themselves as the party was into its second day. There were not only dozens of people but dozens of dogs, including a real lion of a St. Bernard. I couldn't see Tabasco but the guitar player was belting out "Rocky Raccoon."

"I've seen you on TV. Come and join us," called out a tall youth sporting a big red beard and an earring, a rarity at the time. "We're celebrating spring. This is our first barbecue of the season. Help yourself to a steak. Pour yourself a drink."

"Thanks, but I'm looking for a raccoon."

"She's playing pool in the basement. She didn't like the St. Bernard."

With Todd in tow, I followed the sounds of merriment to the basement.

Tabasco was in her element as usual, hamming it up for an appreciative audience. She was up on a table in centre stage position chewing holes in a steak, dunking crackers in the ice barrel and filching ice cubes out of people's drinks. This was one party where she didn't get scolded for doing what comes naturally, like playing feelies in a glass for cherries, lemon slices and celery sticks. At my parties, people didn't like a raccoon pawing their ice cubes. I would offer to give them new ice but they always asked for a whole new drink.

Tabasco wasn't getting into trouble at this party and she wasn't interested in drinking beer, so I let her stay. Todd had just started a huge one-pound steak and a large glass of orange juice and didn't want to leave either. "I'll bring Tabasco home when I've finished eating, okay?"

"Okay, I'll tell your mother where you are."

Gary and Carole were sitting down to hamburgers when I spoke to them through the hole in their screen door, a hole put there by the raccoon, I thought ruefully. "Your son's having steak..."

"Yes, Todd's just phoned to tell us he's out for steak with Tabasco. He thinks that's pretty neat for a nine-year-old," Carole laughed. "He said he and Tabasco are drinking nothing but orange juice. Don't worry. If he's not back in an hour I'll go and get them."

Just after the party incident, Tabasco went away for three days. I missed her. I worried about her. I couldn't concentrate on my work. But I stopped myself from phoning the radio station and asking if somebody had seen her. After all, I told myself, I had given her the choice.

But people phoned me. "Have you lost your raccoon?" asked the man from the bookstore. The lady from the radio station asked, "People have been phoning to get your number. Shall we give it to them?" And Anne from up the hill told me, "The kids at school say some teenagers have Tabasco."

I found out what the raccoon had been up to those three days when two boys brought her home after phoning around town to find out where I lived.

Greg and Hank had picked up Tabasco on the highway. "At first I thought she was a beaver," explained Greg. "She sure plays a lot, she's into everything, she takes everything apart. We took her to the drive-in but she was more interested in eating peanuts and popcorn and exploring the car than looking at the movie."

The boys took Tabasco home to Greg's place. "She chased our friends' cats and hunched herself up like a rabbit whenever she saw a dog so we played it safe and kept our animals away from her. She was very tame and friendly to us though."

"Look at her now," broke in Hank, pointing to Tabasco lying flat out on the chesterfield. "I didn't think she ever slept."

It was a bit hard trying to adapt Tabasco to living on her own because people kept bringing her back. They had the best intentions. They wanted to protect her so they either marched up to the door with her or, if I was away on a cougar hunt or buried in my books, they went around the back and locked her in the cage. Tabasco always seemed to find a way out and, if she didn't, her screams always attracted attention.

And then Tabasco came in heat. I recognized some of

the signs. She was even more active, she wandered more widely. She sniffed where other animals had been. Her nipples enlarged. Yes, Tabasco was now grown up. She was ready to mate and if successful could produce her own family of raccoons.

Unfortunately, other signs of her adulthood caused trouble at home. The raccoon attacked Shelley.

Tabasco was quietly playing on the floor with me when Shelley walked past. Suddenly, she snorted and leapt up to latch onto her arm.

"Get her away," yelled Shelley. "Dad, she bit me."

Down came her father from his den. Shelley was crying and he was angry. "Get that animal out of here," he shouted to me. At the sound of his voice Tabasco fled behind the chesterfield. Knowing that Jack's daughter wasn't hurt, although she was certainly scared, I remained calm, trying to work out why the raccoon had suddenly attacked.

Tabasco acted strange with certain people. Little kids who screamed. Boys who teased. People of a different race and colour than her own human family. Anne up the hill who had once slapped her for making a hole in the screen door. And now Shelley. Did she act differently towards people she wasn't used to? Did she act through jealousy or in defence of me? Or was this sudden behaviour change only because she was in heat?

Jack was a wildlife biologist by profession but he was all parent at the moment. He was not interested in finding answers to my questions. "I don't care," he cried angrily. "Experiment on your own family, not mine."

Quietly, I pulled Tabasco from under the chesterfield and we walked to the creek. Faithful old Beau walked beside us. For an hour, she played in the water on both sides of the creek, she pranced from rock to rock, she turned over pebbles and pulled Beau's tail. Every now and then, she skipped over to me and touched my cheek. I left her there and walked back to the house.

The days passed and the raccoon did not return. I found I had a dull ache in my stomach. I felt that part of me had gone too, even though this was what I had planned. I left the door open at night with the light on, just in case she came back and wanted in. Even Jack was understanding. He left a big bag of dog food out on the porch in case Tabasco came back hungry.

I found it hard to concentrate. I kept wondering what Tabasco might be doing. Had she gone up the creek past the sandhills to the woods? Had she met another raccoon? Had she met a cougar, a coyote or a bear? She had handled domestic animals but could she handle wild ones? These wild animals eat young raccoons. Had she gone down the creek and got run over by a car? A lot of raccoons are run over by cars. I remembered Lino had stopped once to pick up a dead raccoon on the road. He had called it a "Tabasco."

I decided to put a letter in the local papers to let people know about the raccoon. I didn't ask for her to be brought back, just to be told where she was and what she was doing. I did ask to be told if there were problems that I might be able to fix.

Jim, one of the pruners who lived alone in a cabin a

mile or so up the creek, was the only one to call. "She spent a couple of days at my house, walking in and out as she felt like. I put her outside and she slept on the porch. She was no problem to me but she chased the cats. Guess you can't do anything but wait and see if she decides to come back."

"And then what?" Jack reminded me practically. "You realize if she doesn't get bred this time, she'll come into heat again in fifteen days and then what'll you do?"

"I keep telling myself that to be free and wild and take her chances on what might happen is still a better way for Tabasco to live than being locked up in a cage. Raccoons are too intelligent, too curious, too anxious to explore to be imprisoned. I guess I've got to get over this idea that I have to protect her," I shrugged.

On the seventh day, I drew back the curtains in the kitchen and there, sitting on the ground in the cage, was Tabasco. This was surprising. Never before had she entered the cage of her own free will. She looked thin and haggard yet she had not touched her food. She was just sitting quietly on her haunches like a cat. It was a position I had not seen her in before.

The door of the cage was open. Why hadn't she come into the house? Something was wrong.

I ran outside and picked her up. She made a slight attempt to bare her teeth as if she needed to defend herself then cuddled down against my sweater. She was so thin it was obvious she had not been eating well in the wild. I brought her inside the living room to put her on the floor but she clung to me and licked my face.

Beau, whose movements in the house were restricted to the mat by the kitchen door, whined. The furnace came on. The mechanical pruner trundled through the trees in the orchard. Tabasco pricked up her ears to follow each sound. She was alert but there was still something wrong.

I put her down on the floor. She could only crawl.

"Tabasco, what happened to you? You're limping, you're dragging your right leg."

Like an eel, she slithered towards me and tried to climb into my lap. Had she been run over by a car? Or hit by a shovel? I didn't know how far she had gone to get into trouble or what had happened to her, but like a sick dog, she had hobbled home to where she felt safe. And I was glad.

The door opened and Shelley came in.

"Poor Tabasco!" she exclaimed. "Where have you been?" There were no hard feelings on either side. Tabasco ate a sugar cube out of her hands.

Shelley and I drove Tabasco to the vet in Penticton. Dr. Lindsay was a nice young man with blond hair and a quiet voice. "I think she might have fractured her hock but I'll need to X-ray to make sure." He paused.

"What's wrong?" I asked.

"You know, she's an exotic animal and you always take a chance giving one an anaesthetic."

"That's what life's all about, chances. Go ahead and make your own decision."

"Fine. I'll take the X-rays and phone you for permission if I have to put in a steel pin or put her in a cast. One thing more, is she friendly? Does she know her name?"

"She knows her name but only answers it when she wants to. And she is friendly to most people."

I was a bit taken aback when the vet took her away to a cage. I hadn't expected to leave Tabasco with the other domestic animals. I had expected to bring her back for the operation. "Won't you need my help?" I asked. Vets don't normally deal with wild animals. And if Tabasco caused trouble I wanted to be there as backup.

"No, you go on home," he smiled. "It's better to use my own staff and it's better for the animal too."

I spent the next two days thinking about the havoc Tabasco could cause at the vet's clinic despite her impediment. I needn't have worried. Everybody loved her. I walked in to pick her up and she was the centre of attention as usual, stretched out on a white sheepskin rug surrounded by crates of kittens.

"She was no problem at all. So passive. I'm surprised. Raccoons are usually such rambunctious animals," Dr. Lindsay commented.

He said Tabasco had a fractured pelvis. "It must have been done by a car. She couldn't have got it falling. She may have bruised her reproductive or elimination tract but she'll be all right. Bones in young animals are strong. She'll get better eventually but she'll get better faster if you keep her quiet and still in a small space for three weeks minimum."

I groaned, imagining how difficult it would be to keep such a lively, curious creature confined in a small cage for three weeks while her bones mended.

In fact, it was easy. She knew she was hurt. She knew what was good for her. And for three whole weeks she stayed still.

Jack made her a cage on the veranda that wasn't much bigger than she was so she would be forced to stay as still as possible. On the side he attached a water dispenser that chicken farmers use so the raccoon didn't make a mess when she drank. Art Batkin added a heavy board to both the water dispenser and the cage so that Tabasco would not be able to lift anything up or pry anything loose. I put a log down on the veranda outside the cage for visitors to sit on when they came to see how the raccoon was doing.

The one constant visitor was Beauregard. For three weeks, day and night, he stayed by her side. The two animals lay stretched out on their tummies looking at each other, touching noses through the wire. The spaniel was devoted to the raccoon. He moved away only to eat or do his toilet.

Tabasco spent most of the time sleeping. She went back to her babyhood ways, sleeping on her tummy with her head tucked under her front paws and her nose flat on the ground. When I tickled her rhythmically behind the ears or the back of the head, the haws or white slits in her eyes emerged as if she was being lulled to sleep, her lips slucked up and down, and her teeth touching each other made little clacking noises as if she were sucking the milk bottle. This too seemed to be a carry-over from babyhood. Perhaps all creatures act like babies when they are sick.

Whenever Jack was away, which was most of the time, I brought Tabasco into the living room after supper to give her some exercise on the carpet. Poor Beauregard tried creeping in after us, one floorboard at a time, hoping I wouldn't notice, but I steeled myself and told him to stay by the kitchen mat. That's one good thing about domestic animals. They usually do as they are told.

It was about this time that I noticed Tabasco was rubbing herself a lot on the corners of boxes and the hard wooden arms of chesterfields and chairs. She urinated in one of Jack's shoes. One night she got terribly excited and sloshed around in the puddles by the back steps while I was cleaning out her cage. I felt she was coming into heat again. She had the chance to get away but she realized she was still not mended and she stayed. And loyal, long-suffering Beau continued to stay by her side.

Then, exactly three weeks to the day after she came home from the vet, Tabasco decided she'd had enough of sickbed stuff. She must have been back in good shape to get out of the cage—to lift the lid against its lock and squeeze through the gap had to have taken considerable strength and agility. A couple of neighbours phoned to say she was seen around their place but I resisted the temptation to go and get her. Two nights later, she returned. I felt her bones and they were mended. It was uncanny how she knew as well as the vet did that she had healed.

But Tabasco didn't go away again. Perhaps whatever had happened to her during the week she got hurt was so frightening that she didn't want to go back to the wild. In any case, she just resumed her neighbourhood circuit.

She still had her old fans, Gary, Carole, Todd, the Batkins, the Palmbergs, Jim the pruner and the man who had the chickens, but other people didn't want an adult raccoon bothering them, especially in summer when they were working in the orchard or outside their houses. One man complained that Tabasco was taking ice cubes out of his guests' drinks when he gave parties on the patio. The pruners complained the raccoon was climbing their ladders. Soon the pickers would be complaining.

Then Katy Madsen phoned. "We used to enjoy the raccoon coming around but my two girls are frightened to walk home from school now after Tabasco jumped out of the bushes at them. No, she didn't hurt them, but she surprised them."

One lady who liked Tabasco, and sometimes came to put her back in the cage to keep her out of trouble, phoned to tell me what other people were saying. "If you don't mind a bit of advice, I'd suggest you lock the raccoon up. I've heard comments like, 'Well, we're not going to have that animal around this year getting into our gardens.' I'd hate to see Tabasco poisoned like they poison the dogs."

A man building his house phoned to say, "That raccoon is putting his paw prints in my new cement. I threw a shovel at him this time. Next time I'll wring his neck."

Then Jack got an anonymous call at work. "Get that damned raccoon away from my garden or I'll kill it."

There seemed only one thing left to do. After Jack

was called twice from work to pick up Tabasco during the week I was in Toronto on business, he built a new cage, one he hoped that Tabasco couldn't get out of, and he put the raccoon in it.

He told me about it over the phone. "It was four feet high with smooth wooden sides but she jumped out, in fact she flew out. I then put a wire roof on it and that stopped her getting out but I can't stand her chittering. It keeps me awake at night. She is so lonely that I go out and talk softly to her. But all the while, she is growling and snarling and aiming to get at me through the wire. I have to handle her with gloves and a salmon landing net."

When I returned to the Okanagan and saw the cage I could understand why Tabasco was upset. It was like the Black Hole of Calcutta. She couldn't see out except straight up at the wire roof. It was a terrible cell for a creature accustomed to trees and wide open spaces. Even on the balcony of our apartment in the city, Tabasco had a view.

"That raccoon's a monster now, Lyn. You'll have to get rid of it. She's growling and snarling all the time." Without a word, I opened the wooden door and let Tabasco leap into my arms. She purred. "What a monster!" I joked but Jack was not amused.

"She was just being defensive," I tried to explain.

"No, she's offensive," Jack flashed back.

"She's fine with some people but, I agree, not with others."

"I disagree. She's only fine with you. You think your

raccoon can do no wrong."

"I think animals have a special sense that recognizes human feelings towards them. They seem to know when people fear or dislike or resent them and they act accordingly. They show jealousy for instance."

"Are you saying that animals have the same feelings that humans have?"

"In some ways, yes."

"Hogwash."

I sympathized with Jack. He had spent a lot of time and effort in dealing with my raccoon. And he was right, in that Tabasco was now an adult and not afraid of people, so she could be dangerous to those she disliked or who disliked her.

What was I to do? I had promised the people at the Children's Zoo that I wouldn't release Tabasco in an urban area. I couldn't leave Tabasco in a cage. I couldn't leave her loose in the orchard or along the creek even in this rural area. I would have to find another home in the wild for her.

CHAPTER NINE

THERE'S A RACCOON IN MY HEART

I had finished my work in the Okanagan. I was still waiting for a cougar kitten to be born to start my study at the game farm but my cougar studies had finished in the field. Tabasco and I went back to our Burnaby apartment.

Jack came down from Summerland for a visit and Tabasco spent most of her time on the balcony. I bought a new blind to hide her from the neighbours because the old one had been blown to oblivion by the previous winter's storms. It was summer now and too hot to sleep inside with the windows and patio doors closed. I wasn't surprised to return home from university one day to find Jack arranging a wedge at the bottom of the door to keep it ajar to let in air without letting in the raccoon.

"She's been growling and spitting and trying to get at me ever since you left," Jack snapped.

Tabasco remembered who had put her in a cage in the Okanagan. Perhaps she also knew that my university studies were coming to an end and that I was moving to my house in Mill Bay on Vancouver Island. It was on a dead-end street with a stream and trees on one side, a vacant block on the other side and a beach in front—and I dreamed of sharing it with Tabasco. Jack wanted to live there too—but not with a raccoon.

"You can't take Tabasco to Mill Bay," retorted Jack, the scientist. "Your nearest neighbours have immaculate gardens and Tabasco will get herself into more trouble than in the Okanagan. I keep telling you to give the raccoon her freedom. Let her find a mate and lead a life in the wild. Stop being so selfish."

Some of my friends, such as Anne in Summerland and Ernie in Vancouver, agreed but, despite my attempts to release Tabasco in the Okanagan, I never felt in my heart that it was right to release her at all. She was too used to people. To avoid people I'd have to let her go in a remote wilderness and I'd never know then how she'd fare. I felt that because I had raised her I had a responsibility to keep my buddy safe. Besides, the bare patch her surgery had left on her flank had not yet healed. It was red and getting redder as she kept opening up the wound.

I tried to find her a halfway house where she could make her own choice. Lino was the first to offer her a home. He, Paul and Danny had a big house and a swimming pool but it was in a subdivision. Tabasco had already climbed over the fence to the neighbour's pool and frightened her little girl.

Lino suggested his friend Frank, who owned a bookstore in Aldergrove. Tabasco was well used to bookstores. Frank lived beside a gully on a two-and-a-half-acre farm in the Fraser Valley east of Vancouver. The gully was clothed in luxuriant trees, lush ferns and heavily loaded berry bushes. His house was beside a creek and it even had a swimming pool.

His two dogs were playful, friendly spaniel pups but they barked a lot when Tabasco appeared, so Frank put them on a leash. The raccoon must have known something we didn't because she refused to go past the dogs. While we walked the bridge over the creek to get to the house, Tabasco took the culvert route and met us on the other side.

"This is a paradise for Tabasco," said Lino enthusiastically. "There are frogs and fish in the creek, and Frank can feed her all kinds of free meat like mink food. He doesn't have any screen doors for Tabasco to tear off. The neighbours have vegetable gardens but they are retired—one is a minister—and none have said they mind living near a raccoon." I told Frank I would phone when I'd made up my mind.

Strangely, my next offer of a home was on the same street, although streets in Aldergrove can be up to several miles long. Kevin and Erica Robertson lived on twenty acres with a woodsy area in the middle of their hayfield and a mini forest close by. They came to meet us at the gate of the long driveway that led to their house.

As soon as I let Tabasco out of Lino's van, their black Lab bounced up in a boisterous welcome which sent the raccoon up the nearest telephone pole. She didn't dare come down till the dog was out of sight beyond the next bend in the driveway.

But there were other animals to confront before Tabasco could get to the house. A white pony grazing in the field on the side of the driveway saw the raccoon scampering towards him and flicked his ears bolt upright. So did Tabasco when she reached the pony. The little raccoon stretched up as tall as she could above the long grass but still only reached the pony's knee. Tabasco had met a horse before when we went swimming in Sasamat Lake and I had been amazed then how bravely she had stood up to press her nose against the nose of the horse who towered above her. This time, she decided not to make friends with the pony and dashed away to a nearby barn.

The door was closed but she pried open a loose board and came face to face with a black tabby cat bristling with recent motherhood and protective of her litter of kittens. Tabasco usually chased cats because they ran but not this tabby. The newborn kittens tumbled over each other trying to get out of the barn and into a bright new world. They had no idea they would find a masked bandit outside. Fortunately for them, Tabasco met their mother first.

Tabby and Tabasco carefully approached each other to within spitting distance. Each stretched upwards and outwards trying to make herself look more frightening than the other but neither animal would give way. I broke the stalemate by scooping up Tabasco in my arms and leaving Tabby to round up her kittens.

When the chickens loose in the barnyard caught sight of the masked bandit, they scattered to what they hoped would be safety in a half-finished chicken house. They didn't need to worry as the raccoon had never bothered chickens, though she did like eating eggs.

She was more aware of the cows that were now ambling home from the hayfield. They were even bigger than the pony. Instead of passing them to reach the safety of my arms, Tabasco scampered off across the field, scurried under a barbed wire fence and climbed a tree in the surrounding forest. She straddled a limb, all four legs dangling down, with ears perked up and bright eyes alert to what might be coming next. Kevin went inside the house for his camera.

She wouldn't come down till the cows were out of sight and even then I had to carry her in my arms, which is rather hard to do when you are climbing under a barbed wire fence.

In many ways Kevin and Erica's farm was an excellent place to release Tabasco, but they hinted they might sell it and move away someday soon. If that happened, the new owners might not like sharing it with a raccoon.

The next people to offer a home to Tabasco were Jim and Sheila Roberts, who lived in a big house with apple trees and a swimming pool. Their little girl threw all her plastic toys into the pool for Tabasco to play with but their dog Yukon was not so welcoming. He dashed down the stairs from the patio, took a flying leap onto Tabasco's neck and shook her from side to side at least two feet off the ground. I screamed to the rescue. Jim, running beside me, yelled, "Stop!"

Yukon dropped Tabasco just in time. Tabasco's loose

neck fur and Yukon's old teeth had saved her. She shook herself a couple of times then walked sedately away, calmly nosing the grass. Tabasco had come close to death and shown no fear. Nevertheless, I decided she would find no home here. I would have to look farther afield.

The caretaker of the Richmond Nature Park, a boggy area close to Vancouver, invited her to stay there. "I could leave her in the house during the day and let her out at night to meet the other raccoons."

On the day of our visit, Tabasco snatched a bag of chips right from the hand of a little girl walking the board-walk with us. Then she chased the rabbits and squirrels. "She's not staying here," called the warden loudly walking towards us from a considerable distance ahead on the trail. "I've just picked up fourteen mallard ducklings." Tabasco didn't bother chickens but who knew about ducks, especially ducks beloved by the boss. Besides, this nature park was too small and too close to the freeway.

"What about Alouette Lake?" suggested Lino. "It's closer to the wilderness. We can have a picnic while we check it out."

"Great!" said Paul and Danny, always ready to share a picnic with Tabasco.

We left the car in the parking lot of Golden Ears Provincial Park then walked through the bush to the beach. The raccoon followed close on our heels but veered off the trail when she caught a glimpse through the trees of people riding horses along a stream. As our mission was to see how she acted when left free in the wild, I forced myself to let her go and we continued on to find a picnic spot.

We were in the middle of our second helping of barbequed steak cooked by Chef Lino when Paul suddenly pointed to a sandy beach at the edge of the lake some distance away. "There's a bunch of people with cameras standing around watching something. I think they're laughing."

I ran back to where I had last seen Tabasco but she wasn't around. Nor could I find her along the stream. Perhaps she was entertaining people at the lake.

Paul and Danny ran off towards the commotion. "Yes, it's Tabasco," they puffed when they returned. "She's playing with the kids. She likes the attention. She won't come back."

I knew my aim was to leave her but I just couldn't concentrate. What if she hurt someone? "Let's creep up on her and stay still and quiet so she can't see us but we can see what happens."

Lino stayed behind to prepare dessert. Paul, Danny and I hid in the bushes and watched. Tabasco was in full playful show-off mode, dancing in and out of the water, doing her log birling routine, catching slugs, chasing a family of Canada geese on the lake, scampering through her audience, grabbing almost anything that was offered her. She refused crabs but accepted grapes.

The park ranger, probably attracted by the noise, arrived on the scene and chose to give a little talk on raccoons. I could scarcely believe his commentary.

"Yes, it's a wild raccoon. We have a lot of raccoons in the park. I'm surprised this one is out so early; usually they sleep during the day and come out later."

"What's that bare patch on its side?" someone asked.

"It must have been wounded," replied the ranger. "I see your slingshot. You didn't do it, did you?"

"No," said the startled teenager.

"I'm not saying that you did but a slingshot in the park is illegal. You could have done it."

And then the ranger himself did something illegal. He offered Tabasco a sandwich. Mind you, I fed Tabasco and all my friends fed Tabasco when he lived among us as a pet and a companion. But you shouldn't feed animals who live in the wild, and to this ranger Tabasco was a wild raccoon.

By now I realized that I wasn't doing a very good job of finding the right place to release my raccoon, close to wilderness but also close to friendly people and animals who would not harm her. Meanwhile, more tenants were discovering that I had a pet raccoon in a no-pet apartment, Jack was impatient to move to Mill Bay and I had to go north to write stories on Canada's Arctic.

It was while teaching a language arts course at Simon Fraser with Tabasco as the star attraction that I met Lori Putz. "Manfred and I would love to have Tabasco live near us. We live on a one-acre property in Coquitlam by Burke Mountain with bush on three sides and a creek close to the house."

"What are your neighbours like?"

"There are some on the fourth side but you never see them. It's all bush in front of our place on the road side. Tabasco is sure to spend his time at the back side along the creek and facing the mountain and that's all wilderness."

"What if she wants to come inside your house?"

"Well, Manfred's a woodcarver and built our chalet so that it's all enclosed downstairs and mostly windows upstairs. He won't like a raccoon inside, partly because I have allergies. He'll build a little house for Tabasco outside under the roof of his workshop near the main house with a ladder to it so Tabasco's bed would be on the same level as our bed. She wouldn't be able to get to us but she could see us."

Lori's idea sounded worth a try. Manfred got to work and carved a beautiful wooden house for Tabasco on the side of his workshop and attached a carved ladder to the wall to reach it. My niece Julie sent the raccoon a hand-crocheted rug for the floor all the way from Western Australia. Lori put out food and water and some of Tabasco's favourite things.

I phoned Lori the first night from Mill Bay where Jack was enjoying a weekend with me without "that pesky raccoon."

"We had a wonderful time playing with Tabasco till about midnight. Even our in-laws came to join in the fun. We chased each other, played tag and let her play 'feelies' with our hair. We spread ice cubes and Apple Jacks on the lawn and watched her bat them around. We went to bed at two a.m. but kept going downstairs to check on her through the night.

"Tabasco didn't sleep in her new house. Instead, she huddled on the steps by the front door and chirred to come inside. I went to check on her again at five a.m. but she was nowhere to be seen." Lori paused for a moment then added hopefully, "Perhaps she's off somewhere up Burke Mountain."

I spent the following week at university doing my final exams. Lori spent it looking for Tabasco. She spent her days walking for miles around Coquitlam and calling the raccoon's name. She spent her nights outside in a sleeping bag, hoping Tabasco would come back. One night she felt a raccoon circle her bag twice but she had no flashlight to see if it was Tabasco. Another night she came home to see a raccoon disappear under a shed and out the other side to the trees but she couldn't be sure it was Tabasco.

She printed out two hundred flyers and placed them in mailboxes throughout the community.

Dear Neighbours,

Have you seen or made the acquaintance of Tabasco (a female raccoon)? She went missing Friday, June 30, but was seen in the Kingston Street area on Saturday, July 1. Tabasco is very friendly and tame, therefore will follow practically anyone. She is one and a half years old and has a sore spot (non-infectious) on her left side. Until just recently she has lived with Lyn Hancock (wildlife author of *There's a Seal in My Sleeping Bag*, *There's a Raccoon in My Parka* and *Love Affair with a Cougar*).

Tabasco is currently under observation and both Lyn and myself would appreciate hearing

from you if you have any information at all about this raccoon i.e. Where did you see her? Has she met an accidental death? Due to her extremely friendly nature, Tabasco may already have become your family's pet. If so, I hope you'll give her up and phone me anyhow. Thank you very much for taking the time to read this letter and I hope you'll be able to help me.
Sincerely,
Lori Putz

Then Lori added her phone number.

Meanwhile, I alerted the SPCA, the Fish and Wildlife Branch and several newspapers to the fact that Tabasco was missing and listed phone numbers that people could use if they had any information. Every paper put a picture of Tabasco (they called her the Celebrity Raccoon) on the front page.

I joined Lori in the search for news of Tabasco. We tramped all over Burke Mountain, we distributed more flyers, we camped out in our sleeping bags and we even talked to people who had seen her. We learned that Tabasco had not looked for a raccoon buddy in the wilderness. She had looked for human friends in the community.

The ones she found were captivated. One family reported that she had come in through the back door to join their party. I remembered how Tabasco loved being the star attraction of parties. I bet every camera in the room was focused on her when she filched their ice cubes.

Peter Sherrington drove to Lori's house to tell his story: "A raccoon came around to our place and stayed all day. It was the holiday weekend, I think it was Saturday, the first of July. I couldn't get any work out of my boys at all. They went everywhere the raccoon went. They had a real marvellous time. My wife came out and gave the raccoon an egg. It ate that and everything else. At night I didn't want to bring a wild raccoon into the house so we closed the door. I was kind of hoping that it would still be on the doorstep in the morning but it had gone. That raccoon was a real charmer. It must have been Tabasco."

And then we found her ourselves.

On Coast Mountain Road we stopped at a house to give a flyer to a man getting on his motorbike. "I've lost my raccoon…" I began but he wasn't interested. He shoved the leaflet into his pocket and started to rev the engine.

Just then, his son waved from the deck and called out, "My friend's father shot a raccoon on Huber Avenue a few days ago."

I looked at Lori in dismay. Huber Avenue was close to Victoria Drive where Lori lived. Could that have been Tabasco?

"It's the Jobses' place," said the boy before his father told him to go inside.

"I don't know them," said Lori after we thanked the boy and left.

We drove by the Jobses' home but it was late and the house was in darkness. We decided to return early in the morning.

That night I placed my sleeping bag on the lawn at Lori's place underneath the house that Manfred had built for Tabasco, but I couldn't sleep. I prayed that the dead raccoon was not my raccoon, that it was all a mistake.

It was 7:20 a.m. when Lori rang the Jobses' doorbell. I stayed in the car because I knew I would get upset and start saying things I might later regret. A man appeared at the door in his dressing gown.

"We heard that someone shot a raccoon here a few days ago," asked Lori politely. "Do you know anything about it?"

"No," answered Mr. Jobs brusquely. "I'm an animal lover."

Just as he started to close the door, a boy of about fourteen came up behind him. He was in his pyjamas as well.

"Dad!" said the boy vehemently. "You shot a raccoon last Wednesday afternoon with your twenty-two and got me to bury it in the backyard."

I couldn't stay in the car any longer. I ran to the door screaming, "I hate you. You are no animal lover."

"Yes, I am. I love ducks, geese, horses, chickens but I hate raccoons. They have killed chickens, geese and guinea pigs that were our pets," retorted Mr. Jobs defiantly.

Lori and I were both crying but she managed to keep talking. "Can we go and dig it up so we can verify if it really is our raccoon?"

"No, I don't know where it is."

"Your son can tell us." Lori suddenly realized that it was illegal to discharge firearms within city limits and added, "Don't worry. We are only interested in identifying the body. We won't tell the police."

That and our tears seemed to soften Mr. Jobs's hardline attitude. Instead of slamming the door on us, he tried to explain.

"It walked up to us in the middle of the day while we were berry picking in the backyard. My ten-year-old was terrified and ran into the house but the raccoon followed and when the kids kept the door closed, it crawled under the steps and stayed there. My son tried to poke her out with a two-by-four but it still wouldn't leave. Finally, it ran up a tree. We had to take some visitors to the airport but when we returned it was still up the tree. The chickens were running free all over the place but the raccoon didn't even leave the tree to chase the chickens. Another strange thing, it had this patch on its left side. It looked as if it had some disease. And any raccoon that tame must be sick. I thought it had rabies.

"I had to go to work, my wife was already at work, I didn't want to leave my kids home alone with a rabid raccoon, so yes, I shot it. I take full responsibility. I'll find you another one."

That only intensified the tears that were running down my face. Tabasco was dead, not because she was too wild but because she was too tame, and she was tame because that was how I had brought her up. I had to share the responsibility.

"But why didn't you call the RCMP, the SPCA, the Fish and Wildlife Branch, the newspapers? They all knew that a tame raccoon was missing in the neighbourhood.

Somebody could have come and picked her up." Lori was still comparatively calm.

By the tirade that followed, I guessed that Mr. Jobs had little appreciation for people in authority. He was a man who preferred to take matters in his own hands. "I look after myself. I keep a gun at my front door for my protection and that of my family."

Lori tried another tack. "Please tell us where the raccoon is so we can dig her up and leave you alone. Perhaps she isn't Tabasco."

Mr. Jobs would not listen to our entreaties. "I can't remember and neither can my son, and that's that. We're going to have our breakfast. Goodbye!"

The boy tried to intervene but drew back when he saw the stern expression on his father's face.

Just then a girl appeared on the doorstep behind them. She was about ten and was wearing a red dress. "I'll show them, Dad," she said with a sympathetic look in our direction.

Seeing how his own children were almost as upset as we were, Mr. Jobs finally agreed. "All right then," he said in exasperation. "Go get a shovel—and a plastic bag."

Lori followed the children to the edge of their property. I trailed behind, still crying. Tabasco had been my constant companion for over a year and I couldn't bear to think of her as dead.

The boy dug around very gingerly. Lori took the shovel and dug down a foot.

I couldn't stand the waiting any longer. I grabbed the shovel and like some crazy person, Lori told me afterwards, I sent the dirt flying. I dug down another foot.

"There it is." The girl pointed into the hole I made but I couldn't look. I dropped the shovel and walked away. Lori finished the digging. She gently placed the dead raccoon in the plastic bag.

"I don't think it is Tabasco after all," she called to me excitedly. "It doesn't have a bald spot."

My heart leapt. I ran back and knelt down on the ground. I turned the limp body over in my hand and parted the fur. There on the left side was an unmistakable two-inch patch of bare skin with a slight red tinge. We both burst into tears.

We were still crying uncontrollably as we carefully placed Tabasco back in the plastic bag and walked to the car. Back at Lori's place, we buried Tabasco among the trilliums beside a creek that she loved and among the people who loved her.

AFTERMATH

We kept our promise and didn't tell the authorities who shot Tabasco or where she was shot. (It was just a hundred yards through the bush from Lori's.) Tabasco had visited places all over Canada and even parts of the United States. She had charmed people of all ages in parks, schools, bookstores, newspaper offices and radio and television stations. She had her name and her picture in dozens of newspapers and magazines in Canada and in more than two hundred flyers in Coquitlam. It was inevitable that reporters learned about her death and wrote stories about how it happened.

Readers wrote letters to the editor. People wrote letters to me. I was away for several months in the Arctic but Lori kept a file of Tabasco's press clippings. Headlines read "Fear Kills Celebrity Raccoon," "Tabasco Victim of Fear," "Tabasco's Final Chapter One of Fear and Tragedy" and "Pet Raccoon Shot as Thief."

People took sides. Mr. Jobs complained he was being persecuted. He admitted he had a grudge against raccoons but he did say he was sorry he'd shot what turned out to be a tame raccoon, especially such a famous one, and he offered to buy me another one.

Lori tried to be fair. She wrote a letter to the editor of one newspaper to complain that different newspapers had published different versions of the same story and she tried to set the record straight. At first she refused to appear on TV to answer questions but she agreed when the interviewer promised to present both points of view and inform the audience that if viewers had a problem with a raccoon or any animal, tame or wild, they should contact the Society for the Prevention of Cruelty to Animals (SPCA), the Humane Society, the Fish and Wildlife Branch of their provincial government or a conservation officer, and not take matters in their own hands and break the law.

Different places have different laws. In British Columbia, nobody is allowed to capture, keep, poison or kill raccoons without a permit. Raccoons are classified as fur-bearers and licensed hunters and trappers may kill them legally if they follow the regulations. If a raccoon is seriously threatening to hurt somebody, the person with the problem can ask a conservation officer to kill or remove it but if the raccoon is just being a nuisance, the person should ask a licensed hunter, trapper or professional pest control company to kill or remove it. If the raccoon is sick or injured or orphaned, the person who finds it should contact a wildlife rescue organization to treat it and find a suitable place to release it. In British Columbia, this should be as far away from people and buildings as possible. In Ontario, a wildlife rescuer must take it back to the place where it was found.

Over time, society's attitude toward wild animals has changed. Once, governments paid bounties on animals such as wolves and cougars because these were seen as rival predators, competing for the deer humans wanted to hunt and stealing the livestock humans bred for their own use. Seals and whales were destroyed because they ate the fish humans needed. Nowadays, people prefer to live-trap or tranquilize a "problem" animal and release it in another location. The trouble is that although the people feel better because the problem has gone from their own backyard, the animal may die when taken to somebody else's backyard. Another problem is that we are running out of backyards—especially wilderness backyards. Often, an animal finds its way back to people and becomes a problem again.

Fortunately for raccoons, they can adapt to many environments and most can survive on their wits. They are lucky, too. Most people see them as cute, intelligent and a little like humans themselves. I read of one family of raccoons that lined up outside on a patio every night to watch TV through the living room windows. As one with experience, I can believe this story!

I think the best way to avoid problems if you want to share space with raccoons is to learn to live with them. Enjoy them when they visit but anticipate their behaviour. Don't leave food out for them. Guard your doors, windows or pond with an electric fence or mesh-wire screen. Tie your garbage can down and secure the lid with a heavy wire strap or bungee cord. Wrap tin around the trunks of trees and prune overhanging limbs that enable raccoons to enter buildings. Make sure you harvest your fruits and vegetables before the raccoons do.

You may want to get rid of the parent animals if they cause problems, but if you are like most people, you won't want to get rid of the babies. You will want to make them a part of your family, especially if they are orphans, but, unlike domesticated cats and dogs, few wild animals ever make good household pets. They can be tamed but not domesticated. If you keep them in a cage, they will lose the very wildness that attracted you to them in the first place. And you will have to decide which is better, to let them live safely in a prison or take their chances outside.

Would I do things differently if I was given a wild orphan raccoon today? I don't know. Given the circumstances, I think I tried my best to help Tabasco. There are no easy answers when it comes to people and orphaned wild animals. But I do wish I could have done for Tabasco what I did for my first raccoon, Rocky.

I raised Rocky well away from urban areas while I travelled the coast of British Columbia, Yukon and Alaska in a rubber boat. I taught him how to find food along the seashore and in the bush beyond and I released him on one of the Gulf Islands, uninhabited at the time. Many years later, a couple who bought that island read one of my books and invited me to visit. I was thrilled to see so many little raccoons living with them on the island, probably all descendants of Rocky.

I raised Tabasco to live off the land as well but I raised her with people and I released her on the mainland too close to people. When Mr. Jobs killed Tabasco, I was angry, upset and emotional. I reacted with my heart, not my mind. Now I am more understanding. He was reacting with his heart too. He was feeling for his children as I was feeling for my raccoon.

I wrote the story of Tabasco's life in 1978, just after it came to an end. It was not popular in those days to end a story with the death of the hero or heroine. Publishers, parents, teachers, librarians, book reviewers and bookstore owners all wanted happy endings. They told me to tell about the good times and leave out the bad. But I couldn't. You see, I write non-fiction and I believe I must tell my stories as they happened. I don't make up endings in which a wild animal raised with people goes off into the wild where life appears to be perfect, where she meets a partner of her own kind, raises her kids and lives happily ever after.

In his book *Lives of the Hunted*, famous animal writer Ernest Thompson Seton writes, "There is only one way to make an animal's history un-tragic, and that is to stop before the last chapter." So I put Tabasco's story—my diaries, letters, photos, tapes and the book manuscript—into a big box. For twenty-seven years I told stories of Tabasco's life in hundreds of classrooms across the world, to thousands of children. But I always stopped before the last chapter. Until now.

I live on a secluded beach in Nanoose Bay near the city of Nanaimo on Vancouver Island where people are few and wildlife is relatively abundant. Each day wild creatures come to my door. Dozens of birds—chickadees, towhees, sparrows, finches, juncos, wrens, even big flickers—fly in to forage at my feeders. A family of California quail scurries around on the ground beneath the feeders to peck the seeds that the other birds drop. One day a hawk swooped in to scatter the frightened birds and, yes, to my horror, take one off in its talons. Busy little hummingbirds poke their slender bills into the tubular blooms of the tall pink foxgloves. They thrive on the abundant nectar and raise families every year in my garden. But one day I found a newly hatched hummer hanging upside down from a bud in a hanging basket, its tiny feet still clinging to the stalk. Another day, one followed reflected flowers to the patio door and slammed against the glass. I have learned to live and let live. I find it more difficult to live and let die.

Beyond the garden, a river otter emerges from the sea, clambers up the rocks and slithers across the lawn to bed down in the pond lilies. Three times an otter has left a flounder on the red welcome mat at my door. I received them as gifts in return for the koi and trout it has taken from my fish pond.

Six newborn rabbits hop from under the hot tub and scamper over to my newly planted marigolds. One, tamer than the rest, nibbles its way up the new green shoots and buries its quivering little nose into the bright orange petals. "I wish they'd eat my weeds," I wail to my friend. "What's a few flowers compared to these rabbits!" he retorts, entranced by wild creatures cavorting so close to his feet.

I have more animal neighbours in the bay. Great blue herons strut the tide line. Flotillas of Canada geese sail beside them. A pair of bald eagles chitter from their favourite perch atop the ivy-clad fir tree that leans ominously over the beach. Scaups and scoters chase and dive and splash above the tide-covered clam and oyster beds. A seal pops out of the water with a fish and shakes it vigorously from side to side before shlucking it down. Soon it will leave my door to have its pup on one of the little rocky islands at the head of the bay.

It is a place that Tabasco would have loved. A curious thing happened as I was writing the last lines of this book. I walked into the kitchen and there through the patio door I saw a huge raccoon staring at me from the edge of the fish pond. It was the first raccoon I had seen in ten years of living in Nanoose Bay. Perhaps I was wrong about the otter. Perhaps this was the culprit that ate my pond fish. Or perhaps it was Tabasco in another form, thanking me for writing her story.

"Want to raise another raccoon?" my neighbour teases when I rush excitedly to his door to share the news. I am tempted. Yes, I would love to share my home with another raccoon, but despite my private location, the people and busy roads of the city of Nanaimo are not far away. I am privileged to have shared more than a year of my life with Tabasco and I am content to live with my memories. Especially now that Tabasco is alive again in these pages, in words and pictures, in your heart and in mine.

AUTHOR'S ACKNOWLEDGEMENTS

Thirty years have passed since I lived with Tabasco but I cannot forget her. Nobody can. Just like the sauce, she was a peppery character and she added spice to the lives of all who met her.

People loved her, well most people did. I confess there were some who didn't but they still admitted she was charming and they appreciated her amazing agility and remarkable intelligence.

So here's to the memory of Tabasco and thank you to the people who shared your life with her in all the ways I know you remember. Most of you will find yourselves in this book.

Jack and Shelley Bone; Todd and Carole Barrett and Gary Blagbourne; Art, Margaret, Donna and Raymond Batkin; Beauregard; John Britt; Judy Burnell; Anne and Lorne Davidson; Fiona, Bill, Simon and Penny Day; roommates Ellen and Debbie; Frank from Aldergrove; Elizabeth Ghent; Lino, Paul and Danny Gonzato; Carolynn Hastings; Lynn Howard; Jim the pruner; Dr.

Lindsay; Katy Madsen; Walter S. McIlhenny, president of McIlhenny Company that makes Tabasco sauce; Lily Miller, my faithful editor at Jack McClelland's publishing company (Lily and Jack adored Tabasco though in different ways); Yolande Palmberg and family; Grant Parnell; Ernie Perrault; Moira Pitt; Lore and Manfred Putz; Ivy Pye; Con and Dime Reilly; John Richmond; Jim and Sheila Roberts; Kevin and Erica Robertson; Alyce Shearer; Peter Sherrington; my parents, Ted and Doris Taylor; my sister Jan Travia; my niece Julie Travia Craig-Smith; Vera Wilson; Barbara and Bill Zimakas and their family. There were lots more people in Tabasco's life so if you are one of them, write and let me know.

Tabasco's story would have remained on the shelf in a big cardboard box for more than twenty-five years, had it not been for our publicist, Nikki Tate. Nikki, also a writer, listened to me read from the raccoon's story at a party to launch a book called *Readers, Writers, and Recipes*. Tabasco's recipe in that book was called "Tabasco (and Rocky) Raccoon's Clam and Oyster Chowder Made in a Big, Black 20-cup Pot." Nikki was so excited that she told her publisher, Diane Morriss of Sono Nis Press. Diane, remembered from childhood my book *There's a Raccoon in My Parka*, about my first raccoon, Rocky, and she was so excited that she asked if she could publish Tabasco's story.

But there is more. Nikki asked her friend, Loraine Kemp, a wonderful illustrator who loves raccoons, to illustrate Tabasco's book. Diane asked Laura Peetoom, an excellent editor who also loves raccoons, to be our editor.

We all thank Nikki for bringing us together. We had so much fun producing *Tabasco the Saucy Raccoon* that we plan to do more books on my animal companions.

Tabasco is now out of the box, off that shelf, and lives again in the hearts of her readers. We are all excited and we hope you are too.

Lyn Hancock
Lantzville, British Columbia, Canada
December 2005

ILLUSTRATOR'S ACKNOWLEDGEMENTS

Most of the people I'd like to thank either had to model for me and my camera, or help find items needed for my illustrations.

The biggest contributor for my models was undoubtedly the staff and students of Anne McClymont Elementary. The principal, Dr. Sandra Sellick, and the vice-principal, Donna Stathers, were there for poses and support for literally months. The lively enthusiasm of the staff and children made this project an absolute joy.

Many thanks to my writing buddies—Eileen Holland, Mary Ann Thompson, Pat Fraser, Sharon Helberg and Fiona Bayrock—for their encouragement in the early stages.

My devoted family provided assistance during odd hours to either pose or take pictures of me posing in various odd outfits. These helpers included my nieces, Jill, Erin and Katie Wilson, and my sons, Andrew and David Kemp. To my husband, John, an enormous thank you for the countless ways you helped me, and for your unwavering confidence in my abilities.

Sincere thanks go to Mary McCulloch, my artistic mentor, who provided some excellent advice and encouragement, and my good buddy Karen Autio, who provided constant help with poses and advice on the authenticity of the time period.

I would be nowhere without my friend Nikki Tate, who was the one who suggested I send my portfolio to Sono Nis in the first place and mentored me throughout the process, and Diane Morriss, who placed her confidence in me, gave me encouragement and paired me up with Lyn Hancock.

And finally, huge thanks to Lyn Hancock, who after hundreds of lively e-mails, I am honoured to be able to call a friend and partner in this book.

ABOUT THE AUTHOR

LYN HANCOCK has lived with raccoons, cougars, bears, apes, and people, but Tabasco has always had a special place in her heart. Lyn is an entertaining and passionate speaker on the topic that she most enjoys: touching the wild, and letting the wild touch you. Born in Australia, she has travelled extensively in and written about Canada's wild places, particularly the North. Her presentations, classroom visits, and books bring people and nature together and change lives.